What the he[...]

Precariously bal[...]
of the balcony, C[...]
life. Breaking into a cold sweat, she whispered a shaky mantra. "Don't look. Don't think. Just jump."

She took a deep breath, bent her knees and pushed off. A second later her right foot landed on the thin ledge of concrete. As she pulled herself over the rail, she stifled the impulse to laugh. There was nothing even remotely funny about her desperate search for her father. Maybe she'd lost her mind, leaping across people's balconies in the middle of the night. Who did she think she was?

She tiptoed stealthily across the ledge, but just as she had almost reached the opposite side, a shadow moved in her peripheral vision, a dark figure emerging from the room.

"It's you!" Luke's soft, deep voice held as much amusement as incredulity.

Claire smothered a groan. Not him. This had to be a nightmare.

Of all the balconies in the world to get caught on, why did it have to be Luke Dalton's?

TO CATCH A THIEF

BY

DEBRA CARROLL

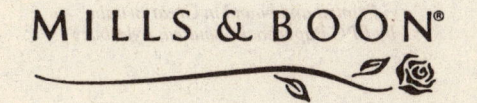

MILLS & BOON

> **DID YOU PURCHASE THIS BOOK WITHOUT A COVER?**
> If you did, you should be aware it is **stolen property** as it was reported
> *unsold and destroyed* by a retailer. Neither the author nor the publisher
> has received any payment for this book.

All the characters in this book have no existence outside the imagination of the author, and have no relation whatsoever to anyone bearing the same name or names. They are not even distantly inspired by any individual known or unknown to the author, and all the incidents are pure invention.

All Rights Reserved including the right of reproduction in whole or in part in any form. This edition is published by arrangement with Harlequin Enterprises II B.V. The text of this publication or any part thereof may not be reproduced or transmitted in any form or by any means, electronic or mechanical, including photocopying, recording, storage in an information retrieval system, or otherwise, without the written permission of the publisher.

This book is sold subject to the condition that it shall not, by way of trade or otherwise, be lent, resold, hired out or otherwise circulated without the prior consent of the publisher in any form of binding or cover other than that in which it is published and without a similar condition including this condition being imposed on the subsequent purchaser.

MILLS & BOON and MILLS & BOON with the Rose Device are registered trademarks of the publisher. TEMPTATION is a registered trademark of Harlequin Enterprises Limited, used under licence.

First published in Great Britain 1996 by Harlequin Mills & Boon Limited, Eton House, 18-24 Paradise Road, Richmond, Surrey TW9 1SR

© Carol Bruce-Thomas and Debra McCarthy-Anderson 1996

ISBN 0 263 80042 3

21-9610

Printed and bound in Great Britain by BPC Paperbacks Limited, Aylesbury

1

CLAIRE HURRIED into the lobby of the Rangoon House Hotel. Inside, she paused and anxiously scanned the vast opulent, central courtyard where shafts of light were playing on the delicately carved Thai columns.

She *had* to find James. Whatever it took she had to find him before he ended up in jail. Or worse, dead.

From what she'd seen so far it definitely wouldn't be easy. All four square miles of Bateaux Island belonged to the huge, exclusive resort. Hotel guests had the option of staying in large, luxurious rooms in the four-story hotel or in secluded cottages tucked away in the tropical greenery on the lush grounds—making it all the more difficult to track down James. Still, that didn't keep her from studying the people in the lobby, half hoping to catch a glimpse of him.

A few people in bright summer cottons stood in front of the registration desk, while others sauntered across the glossy teak floor—every single one of them exuding that sleek, polished perfection that resulted from the best care money could buy.

Trust James to choose this playground of the very rich as the place to get back into business. He always did believe in starting at the top.

Of course, given her luck to date, he wasn't one of the people lounging in the cane chairs and sipping drinks. That would be too much to hope for.

Having focused so intently on just *getting* to this little dot in the Grenadines, she hadn't stopped to consider how she was going to find one man among five hundred guests. A man who did *not* want to be found.

A hard body collided with her from behind. She stumbled forward, then quickly regained her balance.

"I'm terribly sorry. That was very clumsy of me, I hope I didn't hurt you?" a deep, male voice asked.

She looked up into a pair of compelling, pale blue eyes that held hers with a penetratingly direct gaze.

They were the color of Arctic ice under dark, winged brows—and the combination had an unsettling, almost satanic quality. The small smile appearing in their depths made her feel intensely self-conscious.

"No...no, I'm fine." A tiny ripple of anxiety worked its way down to her stomach. "It was my fault for stopping right in front of the doors."

He was tall and dark, except for those curious wolfish eyes, his face all hard planes and angles. An uncompromising face with something almost ruthless about the set of his firm mouth and the deep cleft in his chin that gave him a look of strength and purpose.

"On the contrary, I wasn't watching where I was going." His voice was richly resonant, but she couldn't quite place the soft accent. "Or I would have seen you."

He bared his even white teeth in a slow smile, but his piercing gaze focused on her in deliberate and searching appraisal.

A small warning shiver went through her. She couldn't imagine those pale blue eyes not seeing where they were going. Instinct told her those eyes saw everything. Experience told her to get the hell away from him.

This kind of man generally spelled trouble with a capital *T*. After all, look at James.

"No harm done." She forced a smile.

"Are you sure?" He continued to search her face, a small frown between his dark brows.

"Very sure, thanks," Frustrated with herself, her smile had tightened painfully on her lips. Okay, her mission here might have her rattled but still that was no reason to see something sinister in every stranger. "Excuse me."

She crossed the sunken courtyard, heading for the reception desk, more than slightly relieved to get away from him. He had nothing to do with this business, but at the same time there was something intense... disturbing, about him.

Behind the delicately carved teak counter, a young male clerk greeted her with a gleaming smile. "Good afternoon. How can I help you?"

"Do you have a reservation for Claire Sterling?"

"Yes, Ms. Sterling." She heard keys clicking as he swiftly called up the information on his computer, then said smoothly, "Here we are. And how will you be paying?"

As the printer whirred, Claire pulled her credit card from her purse and laid it down on the glossy polished counter. While the clerk went efficiently about his business, she idly looked over the Batik hangings covering the back wall. And then suddenly she heard the familiar sound of a quiet, authoritative voice.

"I'd like to send a fax, please."

Turning toward the speaker, she saw the man who'd bumped into her standing a few feet away at the end of the reception desk. Surreptitiously, she allowed her glance to travel up the sand-colored pleated pants that hung on his lean hips, over the slightly paler short-sleeved cotton shirt stretched across his broad shoulders, and up to his carved profile.

He was looking down at a paper on the desk, writing something, but even so, she got the strangest feeling that his attention was actually focused on her.

Claire sighed with impatience and turned her gaze back to the clerk. This paranoia was getting out of hand. Overnight she'd gone from being a sane woman to becoming an irrational twit. Guilt, that was the reason. But she couldn't help it, she felt as if James's guilt was written all over her face.

It made her want to hide, but that was ridiculous. Skulking around was a surefire way of drawing people's attention.

Deliberately, she turned her head to glance at the man again, just as he looked up and met her gaze for a moment before turning to the young female clerk who was assisting him.

"Could you send this please? And bill it to my room."

"Certainly, sir. It'll be a few minutes if you care to wait for your confirmation."

With her heart pounding painfully, Claire looked away. His gaze had only met hers for a second, but it was hard, almost accusatory.

For one horrible moment she felt in danger of losing the scanty lunch she'd forced herself to eat. Thank God, the moment passed, but it left her with an ominous feeling that something was going to go terribly wrong.

She squeezed her eyes shut for a moment. She was doing it again, behaving like a fool. She had to get a grip. Yes, the situation was serious, but that was no reason to let her imagination run riot. The man was probably just trying to pick her up.

The thought gave her a giddy sense of relief. Under normal circumstances she would have caught on to that right away, but these weren't normal circumstances. She felt like she'd walked into some paranoid thriller—suspicious of everything and everybody.

Once again she turned and stared back at the man, this time with as much cool control as she could muster, hoping that conveyed her message politely but clearly enough. She wasn't interested.

His deep-set eyes held her gaze for a moment, then he gave a small, amused smile, more a lightening of his expression than a curve to his lips, and a slight nod of his head.

So he was on the make after all. Nothing more sinister than that. And yet there was something knowing in his expression, almost as if he could read her thoughts. A shudder of horror raced through her. Get a grip, she told herself.

She leaned forward toward the clerk and lowered her voice, "Could you please tell me if there's a reservation for James Sterling?"

The man checked his records, "I'm sorry, we have no reservation under that name."

Of course not. The old devil had obviously used an alias. She smiled at the clerk. "I guess he changed his mind."

No point in getting discouraged. She knew this would happen.

Glancing at her watch, she saw that it was already six. That just gave her enough time to unpack and get ready for dinner. He had to eat, and James always went first-class, so tonight she'd go to the hotel's famous five-star dining room. She didn't even want to think about the smaller lounges and bistros dotted around the resort.

She just had to be systematic. After all, he'd only got here yesterday. But, please God, let her find him before he got to work.

"Here you are, Ms. Sterling, if I can just get you to sign this?"

Startled from her dark thoughts, she looked up at the clerk as he passed her a credit card slip, indicating the spot to sign with the pen he held toward her. After scrawling her name with hands that shook a little, she handed it back.

"Okay, then, you're all set." With a smile the young man handed her the key, along with her credit card. "You're in Room 412. Enjoy your stay."

"Thank you."

On her way to the elevators she had to walk right past that annoying man. He stood with one elbow propped on the counter, his long, lean body at ease and yet curiously alert at the same time.

As she went by him she deliberately kept her gaze focused strictly forward. But from the corner of her eye she noticed him turn his head to follow her progress, obviously undaunted by her coolness. To her annoyance she found herself holding her breath. What was it with her today? Normally, she knew how to handle male attention. *Forget him*.

Crossing the lobby, she scanned the face of every man she passed, hoping to see James's familiar roguish features, but with no success. And yet she was still aware of that hard gaze boring into her back. Sick anxiety filled her once again, but this time she ignored it.

It was vitally important to find James as quickly as possible. But in the meantime she had to keep a cool head.

CLAIRE SLIPPED open the top two buttons of her long-sleeved, white cotton shirt. Less than eight hours ago she'd left her home in Toronto in the grip of a damp and frigid February morning. Now she was looking down from the balcony of her room onto manicured lawns bordered by stone pathways that disappeared into verdant tropical foliage. She could see the beach in the distance and the glittering ocean beyond.

Below and to her right lay the swimming pool and the sounds of splashing, laughing people competing with the relaxed rhythm of a steel band playing the "Banana Boat" song. Under a blindingly blue sky, the dazzling tropical sunshine bombarded her senses.

Was she dreaming? The scene was almost impossibly clichéd, like a travel ad come to life. But the heat was oppressive, making her feel hot and confused. And all these happy people were too noisy, making it impossible to think straight. Couldn't they enjoy themselves more quietly?

Oh, God, Claire you're really losing it.

Running a hand through her tangled hair, she lifted it off the damp skin at the back of her neck. What she needed was a nice, cool shower. It would refresh her, clear her head, and she'd be more capable of forming some kind of plan.

Just as she stepped back into the air-conditioned coolness of her room there came a knock at the door.

She felt a sudden rush of hope. Could it be James? Maybe he'd found out from Albert that she was coming after him. Claire crossed quickly to the door and swung it open. Her smile of relief vanished in a surge of anxiety as she met those ice-blue wolf eyes once again.

"You!" The word emerged as a throaty gasp.

He tipped his head to one side, his straight mouth curving in a satiric quirk that made the cleft in his chin more noticeable. His gaze coolly traveled over her face with leisurely scrutiny, lingering on her mouth.

"Yes, me." Despite himself, he couldn't help noticing the damp cotton shirt clinging to her curves and the seductive, tantalizing scent of her perfume.

Danger, his instinct warned.

With her long, tousled blond hair and damp, glowing skin she looked as if she'd just tumbled out of bed after a long afternoon of making love. Very sexy. And no doubt every bit as calculated as everything else about her. He felt suddenly uneasy.

"What can I do to help you?" Her voice was frosty and uninviting.

"It's more what I can do for you."

"Look, I'm sure there are plenty of other women here who'd be interested in a little holiday romance. I'm not one of them. So please go away and stop wasting my time."

In spite of her dishevelment, there was nothing flustered about the cool look of control in her eyes. She was no amateur. For some reason this confirmation of what he already knew left him feeling vaguely disappointed.

"Are you always so presumptuous?"

She blinked. "I beg your pardon?"

It gave him a purely unprofessional spurt of satisfaction to see that he'd rattled her. "I should hope so."

"Look, whoever you are, I'm not interested in what you're selling, so please leave."

Nice recovery and the hauteur was just right. A surge of anger took him by surprise.

"Are you sure about that?" He slowly held up a Canadian passport and flipped it open. "Claire Sterling?" He glanced down at the picture, then up to her face.

"What... do you want?" She'd gone a little pale and nervously pushed the heavy blond hair off her long, slender neck.

"Most people look dreadful in their passport photographs. You're obviously one of the lucky ones." There wasn't much you could do to make this woman look bad. She was beautiful and that went a long way to explaining that poised air. The fact that she was just another thief explained the rest. "Yours is quite good."

"That's my passport!" she gasped, and snatched it from his fingers. Under all that disdain she was awfully tense.

After glancing quickly at the picture to confirm it was hers, her sharp gaze darted over to the tote bag lying on the bed. Her tickets and other papers were still stuck firmly in the side pocket. Clever girl. She knew it couldn't have just fallen out. She was a pro all right.

Her blue eyes leveled on him, filled with suspicion. "How did you get this?"

Instead of immediately answering her question, he stroked his chin meditatively. Now that he knew her state of mind, he could capitalize on it. The thought gave him no pleasure.

"Claire Sterling... Sterling," he repeated. "Means genuine, pure..." The soft pink lips tightened a fraction and her perfect skin seemed a shade paler. She looked like an angel. Only he knew different. "It's amazing how deceiving names can be, hmm?"

"I've never really given it much thought. Now, if you don't mind, I have things to do, so good day," she said dismissively, and went to close the door in his face.

He held it open with one hand. *Not yet, my dear.* "Aren't you going to thank me?"

"What for?" She might look soft and vulnerable, but she was as hard as nails.

"I did return your passport."

She raised her small chin defiantly. "So what! You probably helped yourself to it in the first place."

"What a ridiculous thing to suggest of a complete stranger." He laughed, feeling grim. Naturally she'd be well-versed in the fine art of thievery, but for once he wasn't enjoying this game of cat and mouse. However he'd made her a little nervous and that was exactly how he wanted her.

"This whole conversation has been ridiculous, and I've had enough. Now, if you don't mind, I'd like to unpack." She'd got her nerve back, but the game wasn't over yet.

"Then I'll see you later."

"I doubt it."

"You should never doubt anything I say." He smiled, deliberately making the words sound menacing.

In reply she shut the door firmly in his face.

He stood for a moment, looking at the white-painted, louvered panels. He'd said enough for now. Enough to make her think twice about what she was doing here.

"I'll definitely see you later, Claire Sterling. In fact, I'm afraid we'll be seeing a lot of each other," he murmured, and walked away.

One more bloody complication he didn't need. At times like these he heartily disliked his job.

CLAIRE PAUSED beside a potted fern just inside the entrance to the vast, elegant dining room. More Thai columns supported a ceiling painted to resemble a forest canopy.

She surveyed the black-tie crowd with a trace of contempt. The idle rich at idle play. These kinds of people had always been part of her life; in her job she dealt with them constantly. Outwardly, she knew that she fit in, but that had nothing to do with her real self.

If she'd come here for a holiday of her own choice, she would much rather rent her own private island. Just her, the sand and the sea, and a beautiful view everywhere she looked. But most of all, peace and quiet.

But here jewels glittered, and crystal and silver gleamed in the subdued light. Intent on her search, she looked around in dismay at the sea of faces. Across the expanse of small tables and snowy linen, it was difficult to distinguish individuals, but surely she'd recognize James, even in this crowd.

A waiter sped quickly past in his immaculate white jacket, carrying a silver tray laden with steaming seafood that sent tantalizing aromas wafting up to her. Her stomach tightened with a loud grumble and she put a hand on her midriff. She hadn't eaten for hours, not since the plane. A good meal would go a long way to restoring her equilibrium.

"All by yourself?"

She started at the sound of the voice beside her. It was only the maître d', his smile a harmless flash of white teeth lighting his ebony face.

She was so on edge she was ready to explode. Better calm down. If she was going to succeed in finding James, she'd better use her wits, not give in to her nerves.

"Yes, just one."

He clucked and shook his head. "We'll have to do something about that," he said in the soft island lilt.

As he led her on a winding path through the tables she carefully scanned the faces she passed, but with so many it was hard to focus on individuals.

Stopping at a large round table where five other people were already seated, he pulled out the remaining empty chair. "Here you are."

Just as she went to lower herself into her seat, she glanced through the diners and caught sight of the man who had stolen her passport, only two tables away.

It couldn't be. Her stomach lurched and this time it had nothing to do with hunger. Here she was, worried sick about finding one man, and she couldn't get rid of another.

Steeling herself, she met those translucent eyes that held a dark smile in their depths.

She swallowed hard. He was dressed in black-tie and looked saturnine and dangerous. Against the crisp white shirt his tanned skin was a rich, golden color.

"Yes, it's me," his smile seemed to say, and there was an element of mockery in his expression. He was enjoying her discomfort.

All at once she became aware that the waiter was still holding out her chair and that the other five people at the table were staring at her with open curiosity.

If she'd set out to draw attention to herself she couldn't have done a better job. She quickly dropped into the chair and the waiter pushed it closer to the table.

"Enjoy your dinner." With a broad smile he hurried away.

The petite blonde on her right spoke up first. "Hi, I'm Nikki Jones."

"Claire Sterling, nice to meet you." Had she seen a subtle sharpening of Nikki's expression, as if in recognition? *Oh, no, here I go again.*

The young American smiled. "Nice to meet you, too."

Across the table a dark-haired older woman, beautifully dressed in a cream shantung Chanel jacket, also smiled at Claire. "I'm Maisie Fleming and this is my husband Morris...Morris, say hello to Claire Sterling," she finished loudly, leaning toward her husband to speak directly into his ear.

Morris adjusted his glasses with one gnarled, unsteady hand and smiled vaguely and rather sweetly in Nikki's direction.

"Good evening." He bobbed his head up and down. "Welcome aboard."

"No, dear." Maisie's slightly shrill voice held only patient good humor. "That's Nikki." She put a hand to his chin to gently turn his head and tiny fireworks coruscated from her diamond cuff bracelet. "That's Claire over there."

Morris's faded blue eyes peered at her through thick lenses, then he smiled. "Welcome, my dear."

Claire warmed to his innate gentleness. "Nice to meet you."

Maisie sat back and folded her hands on the table, looking pleased. An elegant and very handsome woman, probably in her fifties, she dressed in perfect taste and wore absolutely magnificent jewels.

Claire appraised the bracelet and matching earrings with an expert eye, recognizing the Cartier design. Strands of smaller linked diamonds formed an impressive cuff, set with two rows of emerald-cut, two-carat stones. Probably a cool half-million dollars on her wrist alone.

"I'm Steve," the young man next to Maisie added. "And this is my wife Helen." He turned to smile sheepishly at the extremely young woman at his side and caught her fingers in his.

"We're from Buffalo, New York." Helen smiled and squirmed, turning to gaze lovingly at her husband as his hand wandered to the nape of her neck.

Nikki leaned over and spoke softly out of the side of her mouth. "They've been like that since they got here, nauseating isn't it?"

Claire glanced quickly at the couple to see if they'd heard, and felt relieved to find them absorbed in each other. "I don't know, I think it's rather sweet and very romantic."

In spite of her own ill-fated experiences, she still believed in the power of love to make one's life complete. And it was refreshing to see unaffected people who weren't ashamed to express their feelings.

"Is that what you're here for...romance?" Nikki cocked her head and gave a cynical grin.

"Not me, thank you," Claire said emphatically. Too emphatically. She noticed the other woman's green eyes narrow with curiosity.

"Why not? That's what most single people are after here."

"Including you?" she shot back archly.

Nikki laughed and shook her head, then sobered, her expression purposeful. "Not me...uh-uh. I'm here for the fishing."

Claire blinked in surprise. "Fishing?"

"Yeah, there are some big fish in these waters and I plan on getting me one."

She eyed Nikki doubtfully. The other woman's strapless, hot-pink dress revealed the toned arms and shoulders of an athlete, but she was tiny. It was hard to picture her hauling in a marlin.

"So what *are* you here for?" Nikki persisted.

"Just some rest and relaxation." She was a hopeless liar. No doubt it was her own guilty conscience that had put that masked skepticism on the other woman's face.

As dinner proceeded it was no surprise to find that Nikki came from California. With her vivacious personality, sun-bleached blond hair and golden tan, she seemed every inch the beach girl.

And Maisie took great pride in telling her all about Morris's very successful insurance company, now being run by their son. They took a Caribbean holiday every winter, she told Claire, because much as she and Morris loved their home near Chicago, the warm weather was good for his health.

Was this the typical second marriage of a wealthy man to a beautiful and much younger wife? She saw it often enough among the rich, and rather despised the phenomenon. But if that was the case with the Flemings, then Morris had found himself a gem.

Despite her shrill manner of speech, Maisie was the soul of tact and patience, guiding her sometimes confused elderly husband through the meal with unfailing good humor, giving him conversational cues and repeating comments he'd missed.

But not for one moment could Claire forget the man sitting only a few tables away. Somehow he was out of place. He didn't look like a man who wasted his time lying around sunbathing.

Without even looking she could *feel* his gaze burning into her, and then a sudden wave of heat would suffuse her body.

Worst of all, his constant scrutiny had been so distracting that she'd forgotten to look around for James. But surely she couldn't have missed his tall, distinguished figure?

As soon as decently possible, she finished her coffee and gently refused Maisie's good-natured invitation to join her and Morris in sampling the resort nightlife. She told them that she was tired and going back upstairs to her room.

Once out of the dining room she headed for the casino. Passing quickly through the noisy room, Claire surveyed the groups of elegantly dressed men and women clustered around the roulette and baccarat tables. James wasn't there.

Out on the patio it was blessedly quiet, the air was balmy but fresh. The pool glowed like an aqua jewel in the darkness. Strings of Japanese lanterns cast little trails of colored light onto the shifting surface of the water.

Away from the pool silvery moonlight gilded the palms and left shadowy corners where a few couples nestled close on deck chairs, their soft murmurs carried to her on the scented breeze.

Claire tried to glide unobtrusively past while looking them over carefully, without seeming like a voyeur. It was not unlikely some woman had latched onto James. He was a good-looking and extremely charismatic man. But he wasn't among the couples.

After an exhaustive search of the other lounges she dragged herself back to her room, exhausted and discouraged.

For a moment she stepped out onto the balcony to get some fresh air and try to unwind. Leaning on the railing, she took a deep breath of the balmy air, caught, almost against her will, by the spell of the tropical night.

A three-quarter moon rode high in the velvety sky, studded with a blaze of stars. Above the constant sigh of the ocean she could hear the faint dry rattle of the palm leaves carried to her on the soft breeze.

In the distance she could vaguely make out a few figures on the beach and the gleam of foaming waves. The night was so incredibly beautiful. And suddenly there were tears in her eyes and she felt utterly helpless and scared. She loved James so much. If anything were to happen to him, how would she go on?

She dashed the tears from her eyes. This wasn't helping at all. She turned away from the romantic scenery. Off to her right, near the end of the row of balconies, a movement caught her eye, a figure dressed in black sliding off the roof to hang suspended for a moment in midair.

James! She almost yelled out to him, but bit back the words just in time. The last thing she wanted to do was attract attention, but more importantly she couldn't risk startling him. He could miss his footing and fall to his death.

It was fourteen years since he'd pulled his last heist. He was fourteen years older, out of practice, and out of condition. With her heart in her mouth, she watched him drop lightly onto the balcony below.

Frantically, she waved her arms. "James! James!" she whispered, as loudly as she dared, but he made no response and she knew he couldn't hear her.

As she watched, he opened the door and vanished into the room. What should she do? In the dark she'd tried to hastily count the balconies and thought the room was either six or seven away from hers, but she wasn't sure and she could hardly go along the corridor, knocking on doors at one in the morning.

But she had to stop him, and there wasn't a moment to lose.

With only a quick glance at the huge gap between her balcony and the next, Claire hitched her short black dress up around her hips, kicked off her shoes and climbed over the railing.

2

PRECARIOUSLY balanced on the narrow outer ledge, Claire clung to the wrought-iron rail for dear life. What the hell was she doing?

She couldn't help taking a quick look down to the dark bushes dreadfully far below. She jerked her head up, trying to control her shaking as she assessed the distance to the other balcony.

Could she just stretch across and grab onto the other railing before letting go of this one? Squeezing the cold metal tightly in her sweaty left hand, she leaned forward and reached out with the other, stretching with all her might across the yawning gap. Her fingers clawed the air in vain. No, this wasn't going to work.

She pulled back, trembling, knowing she had no alternative now. Breaking into a cold sweat, she closed her eyes for a moment and whispered a shaky mantra. "Don't look. Don't think. Just jump."

Quivering with fear, she took a deep breath, bent her knees and pushed off.

A second later her right foot landed on the thin ledge of concrete. Clutching for the iron railing, she hung on tight and let out a small sob of pure terror. She'd made it! Weak with relief, she straightened and willed her legs to stop trembling.

That hadn't been so hard, not really.

Forcing herself to move, she climbed over the rail and tiptoed across the balcony, her bare feet crunching on the rush matting that covered the concrete. She cringed at the noise. It sounded loud enough to wake the dead. Keeping one eye on the closed sliding door, she crossed to the other side. All she needed was for the occupant to come out and find her here.

Licking her parched lips, she steadfastly straddled the other rail and stood trembling on the ledge once more, trying to get her breathing under control. Again she found her gaze inexorably pulled to the black depths at her feet.

I could die tonight.

She quickly brushed the thought aside. "Stop being so hysterical," she muttered under her breath. "You did it once, you can do it again. Just jump."

She leapt across the gap and smashed her knee into one of the wrought-iron bars. When searing pain shot up her leg, she gasped and her foot slipped. Yelping in panic, she grabbed for the railing, wrapping her fingers around it and hanging on for all she was worth. She crouched there a moment, her eyes squeezed shut, with one leg dangling off the rough concrete ledge. No more thinking about dying. It was making her clumsy.

From nowhere came the hysterical urge to laugh. She stifled the impulse. There was nothing even remotely funny about this. Maybe she'd lost her mind, leaping across people's balconies in the middle of the night. Who did she think she was, Emma Peel? But this was no time to question her sanity, she had to hurry.

As quietly as her tortured breathing and trembling legs would allow, she climbed over the railing, then froze. On this balcony the sliding door stood open and the breeze sent the white curtains billowing into the darkened room, but there was no light and no movement inside.

She tiptoed stealthily across, but just as she reached the opposite railing a shadow moved in her peripheral vision, a dark figure emerging from the room. She heard a sharp intake of breath, and froze.

"It's you!" His soft, deep voice held as much amusement as incredulity.

She turned and smothered a groan. No. Not him. This had to be a nightmare.

Of all the balconies in the world to get caught on, why did it have to be *his*?

"Hello." Inane as that sounded, she didn't quite know what else to say. She was almost surprised that her voice still worked. "I suppose you must be wondering what I'm doing here." *I know I am*.

He stepped clear of the billowing curtains and stood in front of her, a small smile curving his lips.

"No, I'm flattered by the trouble you went through to see me. You could have just come to my door." He was dressed entirely in black, his shirt open at the neck.

"Obviously I'm not here to see you," she snapped. She wasn't in the mood for this man's stupid games right now.

"Oh?" He looked crestfallen. "I'm devastated." But she could see the amusement in his eyes, hear it in his deep, husky voice.

"I'm sure you'll survive."

Please, God, don't let him ask why she *was* here. What could she possibly say to get herself out of this one?

"Who's the lucky chap?"

For a moment she barely registered what he'd said. Then relief zinged through her, leaving her as insanely lighthearted as she had been desperate a moment ago.

Perfect, why not? The worst he could think was that she was oversexed and foolhardy. But she couldn't let him see her relief. He was too astute.

Feigning coyness, she looked down, but continued to watch him intently through her lashes, as if he were a cobra poised to strike.

"Now that would be telling, wouldn't it?" She hadn't meant to sound quite so provocative.

As she held her breath he gave her a long, steady look. Then a sultry smile curved his mouth. She caught her bottom lip between her teeth. What was he going to do now? She didn't know what to expect from this man.

He slowly moved closer, his deep, velvet voice a seductive murmur. "He must be very special, to risk your life and limb like that."

There was something predatory about his soft tread. She sidled away, every muscle tensed to flee. "He is," she said a little wildly. Well, at least that was the truth.

For a long moment he looked at her, his hands pushed into his trouser pockets, his lean body at ease, but with that air of alertness she was beginning to recognize, as if he could spring into action at any second.

She could almost feel his penetrating gaze boring into her and she had to steel herself not to back away even farther. Some instinct she barely recognized told her that she couldn't let him see how he intimidated her. She stood her ground, trying to ignore the sound of her pulse pounding in her ears.

"Call me crazy, but I'm jealous."

"You're crazy, all right, and so am I to stand here talking to you."

She should turn and walk away right now, but she couldn't take her eyes off him. Off his supple, lean body, the long legs encased in black, hip-hugging pants, the broad shoulders, the hard curve of his throat exposed by the open-necked shirt, the strong chin with that determined cleft and his enticing eyes.

Everything about him was so powerful, so masculine, so sexual, so *dangerous*. It permeated his every movement, every action. Would it be there in his kiss?

The thought sent a terrifying surge of heat pulsing between her thighs. Her breasts felt suddenly heavy, the nipples tightening, aching.

I want him. The realization slammed into her like a locomotive, taking her breath away.

She swiveled abruptly away and began to retrace her steps on shaky legs.

"Where are you going?" he asked, his tone ironic.

"Back to my room." She approached the dreaded railing weak with relief that she hadn't given herself away.

"But what about Mr. Right anxiously waiting for you?"

"He'll have to keep waiting." Her voice shook with tension. "I'm not in the mood anymore."

"Poor man. I hope it wasn't anything *I* said?"

"I wouldn't lose any sleep over it."

Not daring to look at him, she climbed back over the rail and turned to make the jump, her bare toes gripping the concrete ledge again.

The leap across held no fears for her now. This time she was more worried about the danger behind her than the risk of death in front.

An instant later his hard fingers curled around her elbow in a viselike grip. "Please, I couldn't bear it if you fell." He must have closed the distance between them with catlike speed and silence. "Won't you use my front door instead?"

His warm breath fanned her cheek and she could feel the heat of him close behind her. Her trembling increased and she closed her eyes for a moment, shocked to the core by the overwhelming urge to just lean against him and feel the hard length of his body against hers.

It took every ounce of reason and willpower to hold herself stiff. She could only thank God that he couldn't see her face right now.

"Come, Claire, let me help you." The gentleness in his voice didn't reassure her when she could feel the strength in those fingers wrapped tightly around her arm.

Mortified to the bone and unable to look at him, she forced herself to turn. It was an effort to lift her leg and he must have realized how shaky she was because the next moment he put his arms around her and lifted her over as if she weighed nothing.

As soon as her feet touched the rush matting he let her go, but rested his hands on the railing on either side of her. Now she was trapped between his tall, warm body and the cool, hard edge of the wrought iron.

He was so close she could smell the faint, not unpleasant whiff of brandy on his warm breath. He was so close that the heat of his body singed hers all the way down, making every nerve-end on the surface of her skin sing with awareness.

It was absolutely impossible to look up and meet those knowing eyes. She dropped her gaze and saw that the skirt of her fitted black dress was still hiked up around her hips, revealing the high-cut, lacy leg of her black panties.

The discovery left her numb. At this point she was beyond being further mortified. With slow, automatic movements she pulled down the clinging fabric.

For eons it seemed she stood there. The moments ticked by and she became aware of the sweet scent of jasmine on the warm night air, the chirp of crickets, the rhythmic sound of his slow, steady breathing.

Finally she lifted her gaze. Pale moonlight caught his face, grazing the high cheekbones. A face like that of some ancient warrior carved in marble. And then she met his eyes, glittering in the silvery light, searching out her secrets.

Her voice emerged in a cracked whisper. "Why are you looking at me like that?"

"You're very nice to look at." His deep voice was soft and resonant in the darkness. So intimate, only she could hear it. So calculated, it must work every time.

"Thank you for the compliment. I'm flattered. I'm also very tired and I'd like to go now." She heard the desperation in her voice and knew he must have heard it, too.

He didn't move, but somehow he was closer, his lips tantalizing inches away. Nothing moved, no one breathed, time stood still. All she had to do was raise her face a little. Something in his eyes compelled her, as if by sheer will he could bring her to him.

She tore her gaze away, down toward the aquamarine rectangle of the swimming pool far below. Anything to escape that inexorable seduction, that piercing examination.

Down by the pool she noticed a man skirting the darkened patio. Despite her panicked state, something vaguely familiar about him pricked at her. As he passed under one of the Japanese lanterns he turned and looked up. It was James!

Claire gasped and her heart began pounding with fear. She glanced quickly back up to her companion. To her relief, his gaze was still fixed on her face. But she noticed that he'd removed one hand from the rail, leaving her free to escape.

She quickly stepped away from him, feeling suddenly far more in control. "Thank you. Good night," she said hastily, and darted away.

"You're welcome." His soft husky voice followed her through his room as she headed toward the door.

The soft lights in the hallway seemed dazzling after the moon-silvered darkness. She blinked and looked around for the nearest exit, then propelled herself frantically down the stairs to the ground floor.

Once outside, she listened for a moment before making her way to the pool, keeping in the shadows. Before stepping into the light she darted a look toward his balcony and saw that it was empty. Thank goodness.

Now she was away from him she could think more clearly. Thank God, he'd allowed her to escape, but she was left shaken to the core by that overwhelming hunger for a complete stranger. She'd never felt that way before, not even with the man she'd been in love with, shared her life with.

But that was over, and right now she had something more important to occupy her.

Overhead, the Japanese lanterns were swaying in the breeze as she hurried anxiously around the deserted deck to the other side of the pool. There was no one to be seen, but she could hear faint voices coming from the casino terrace behind the shrubbery.

Darting down one of the paths that bordered the pool she whispered as loudly as she dared, "James!" Only the soft swish of the breeze in the palm fronds and the sighing of the waves could be heard. "I know you're here, you devil. Where are you?"

But there was no sign of him. She cursed, spun around to retrace her steps and collided with the man standing right behind her.

Reeling back from the impact, she saw a good-natured male face beaming up at her from beneath a thatch of curly brown hair.

"Hi, there, honey. Feel like some company?"

"Not tonight, I'm afraid." She tried to brush past him, but he blocked the narrow path.

The unfastened bow tie of his tuxedo hung askew and in one hand her would-be swain held two full glasses of champagne, the liquid sloshing back and forth as he swayed unsteadily.

"Aw, come on." He tried to press one of the glasses into her hand, but she held up a palm to ward it off. "One little drinkie won't hurt. I don't bite."

She quelled the urge to flatten the guy. The main thing was to get rid of him, so she could continue her search. "No, really. I don't drink . . ."

"Look, I see you standing out here all by yourself and I said to myself, 'Howie, a beautiful woman like that shouldn't be alone. Go make friends.'" He leaned toward her and the scent of his heavy, sweet cologne mingled with the champagne on his breath was nauseating.

"No, really, Howie. I appreciate the gesture, but I'd rather be alone right now."

"I can't let you do that. No, sir, I can't let you do that." He draped a heavy arm around her shoulder, his head practically resting on her collarbone. "There's a law on this island, you know. You can't spend moonlit nights alone."

She struggled to disengage one clammy paw from her shoulder. This was becoming annoying. "Yes, I can... Believe me, I prefer it that way."

"Hey, you can't pay all this money to come here and be alone," he cajoled. "I can show you a good time. A little dancing, maybe a little casino, what d'ya say?"

"Take a hike." The deep, quiet voice that she was beginning to know so well cut through the darkness behind her.

The drunken good humor on Howie's face evaporated as he stared past her. "Hey, buddy, I didn't mean any harm, really. Didn't know the lady was with somebody." He withdrew his arm. "Just being friendly."

With a nervous laugh he backed off, then beat a hasty retreat, the champagne spilling over the glasses as he hurried unsteadily away along the path leading back to the casino.

He could read her unwillingness to turn and face him in every line of her sinuous body. With her hair pulled back, the moonlight sculpted her finely boned face, turning her skin to pale, smooth alabaster. He had to resist the powerful urge to reach out and stroke her cheek.

"This island is just full of people trying to be friendly, isn't it?" She gave a small laugh and it wasn't hard to see her nervousness. Her eyes looked so big, so luminous, so disturbed.

He had an uneasy gut feeling, a premonition of disaster that made the muscles tense in the back of his neck. He flexed his shoulders to ease the tension. He'd learned never to ignore his instincts.

"I know I'm no more welcome than he is, but I thought you could use a helping hand."

Her mouth curved in a trembling smile and once again he felt the same inconvenient surge of desire that had taken him by surprise on his balcony. Desire was a luxury he couldn't afford.

"Well, good night." He'd spent enough time with Claire Sterling tonight. He turned and began to walk away.

"Thank you for helping me out just now." Her soft, hesitant voice made him slow down. "And thank you for returning my passport. I'm sorry I accused you of stealing it."

"I did." What the hell was the matter with him? Why had he blurted that out?

"You did what?"

He turned slowly toward her. "I stole it."

"Why?" she whispered. She looked fragile under the soft-colored lights of the lanterns. Vulnerable.

Once again he felt that dangerous mixture of hunger and protectiveness. No, this couldn't be happening to him. Any fool should be able to see through her routine.

His voice came out a little harder. "Because I wanted to meet you."

"You needn't have gone to so much trouble just for that," she said quietly.

Claire knew she should be feeling relieved. After all, he'd dispelled her lingering fear that he somehow knew why she was here, that he could see her guilt. But instead of relief she felt a trembling excitement, unreasonable and dangerous.

"No?" He tilted his head to the side, in that way she was coming to know so well, and pinned her with a long, assessing look. "Somehow I thought I would."

"You were wrong." She tried to make her voice firm and cool. "But I think it only fair to tell you that I don't believe in casual sex, so if that's what you have in mind, don't waste your time on me." Besides, she had no time to waste herself. She wasn't here for a holiday. But if she were... She might be very tempted.

"There you go presuming again. Who said anything about sex?" He gave her an admonishing smile and his eyes gleamed with provocative humor. "Why don't you wait until you're asked?"

She stiffened, then tried to mask her embarrassment with indifference. But her frosty glare had no effect whatsoever. If anything, the slight curve of his lips only deepened with a devilish amusement that was becoming all too familiar.

"Good night Mr.—" She broke off, confused. She didn't even know his name!

"Dalton. Luke Dalton."

The name suited him, hard and uncompromising. "Good night, Mr. Dalton." She spun away.

"You can't make indecent propositions to me one moment and call me *Mr.* Dalton the next. Come on..." His voice was soft and coaxing, but filled with wicked humor. "Call me Luke."

"When hell freezes," she flung over her shoulder, trying for scorn.

He laughed, soft, deep and low. "I think we're in for a change in the weather. Good night, Claire."

She quickened her pace as she walked toward the hotel, alarmed to find herself trembling. Damn that man!

A PIERCING SCREAM brought Claire bolt upright in bed. Another scream had her wide awake and scrambling to her feet. A quick glance at the bedside clock showed that it was almost 7:00 a.m. even as the next scream had her lunging for the door.

Was the hotel on fire? Was someone being murdered? As she dashed out into the hall she heard other doors opening, heads peering out and a swelling murmur of voices.

Down the corridor she saw Maisie standing in her open doorway dressed in a black silk wrapper with tears streaming down her distraught face.

Oh, no, could it be Morris? Claire rushed down the hall. "What's the matter? What's happened?"

She took the older woman's outstretched hands in hers and found them cold and shaking.

Maisie clutched her tightly, babbling incoherently as she pulled her into the room. For a moment Claire hesitated, steeling herself to face the worst.

But Morris was sitting on the side of the bed, looking dazed, but very much alive, while an agitated Maisie wrung her hands and moaned, "What are we going to do? Where could they be?"

Claire frowned in confusion. "Maisie, what's wrong?"

"My diamonds, my beautiful diamonds, they're gone. They've been stolen!" she wailed.

"Stolen?" Claire felt like she'd been turned to stone.

Even though it was the reason she'd come to Bateaux, for the first time in her life James's former profession became real to her, not just some long-ago fairy story.

Although she knew the truth only too well, she couldn't help asking, "Are you sure?"

"Yes, dear. After the first robbery, I wasn't taking any chances. I put them under my pillow. I thought they'd be safe there."

The first robbery? How many others had that low-down sneak perpetrated?

Her mind spun in terrible circles, barely aware of Maisie's pitiful wailing and Morris just sitting there watching, his old eyes filled with helpless confusion.

"I understand you've had some trouble."

A crowd had gathered at the door and it parted to admit a small, gray-haired man whose impeccable cream suit and take-charge air made it clear that he was hotel management. Oh, God, there'd be security staff, probably the police involved, too!

Maisie rushed forward and began telling the man what had happened. Claire heard her teary, agitated story with growing horror. How could James do this? And to Maisie, of all people. Now, more than ever, she had to find him and make him give back everything he'd stolen.

It was one thing to glamorize his past profession when it was just a story. But it wasn't a story anymore.

In turmoil, Claire pushed her way out of the room, past pajama-clad guests wondering what had happened.

As she ran down the corridor a door opened and she came face-to-face with Luke Dalton. He was freshly showered and shaved, looking very tanned and fit in navy slacks and a fine, white cotton shirt with the sleeves rolled up.

"Good morning." His gaze ran quickly over her and flared in hot appreciation. She suddenly realized that she was wearing only the thin, white cotton T-shirt in which she'd slept, barely covering the top of her thighs. "What's happened? What's all the fuss about?"

After that brief, heated look, his eyes had never strayed from her face, but nevertheless she wrapped her arms around herself, terrified her body would betray her.

"Poor Mrs. Fleming had her jewelry stolen." Feeling intensely self-conscious, Claire could hardly get the words out.

Whatever she had run from last night, it wasn't just a thing of moonlight and magic, it was still very much in evidence this morning.

"Poor Mrs. Fleming." The words were commiserating, but they were at odds with the sudden hardness in his voice. A flicker of anger crossed his face.

She felt confused by his response, confused by her body's betrayal of her, and at the same time suddenly remembered that she shouldn't be standing here talking.

This was no time to waste her energy trying to figure out what was going through Luke Dalton's head. She had to concentrate on finding James, now more than ever.

"Excuse me." As she went to brush past him, his hand shot out to gently but firmly cup her elbow.

"Just a minute, Claire." He paused, intent and serious as he examined her face. "I'd like to apologize for being such a—bastard?—last night. I was insufferable, and I'm sorry."

She was surprised to see his eyes darken with sincerity.

"Don't worry about it. It's already forgotten." An alarm sounded in her fevered brain. If anything, he was even more dangerous to her in this gentler mood. She tried to continue on her way, but he kept a hold on her arm.

"You know, he's not worth it," he said quietly.

She looked up at him warily. "Who's not worth it?"

"This guy you were risking life and limb for. He's not worth it."

"You don't know what you're talking about." She tossed it off flippantly. She couldn't get into this, couldn't cope with telling any more lies.

He raised a hand and slowly trailed his fingertips down her cheek, the feather-light touch tingling across her skin and suddenly making her breathless.

"Just give me a chance," he murmured, his gaze lingering on her mouth.

For a moment she was caught, captivated by the mesmerizing sensuality burning deep in those blue eyes.

She had to get away, and the sudden urgency of that need had nothing to do with James or the disappearance of Maisie's diamonds.

Something deep inside her responded to something in him in the most elemental, inexplicable way. It had kept her awake for the better part of the night and it terrified her.

"Look . . ." she began, then trailed off at a loss for words as he tilted his head expectantly.

What could she possibly do? Tell him the truth? That she wasn't here for a holiday in the sun. That she had to find a jewel thief and make him return his stolen goods?

The trouble was that glib excuses didn't come easily to her. And they didn't work on him.

"I'm not interested in you," she said finally. "I don't want to see you. And I can't be any more honest than that."

His dark, slanted brows rose a little in surprise and he gave her a long, enigmatic look before saying slowly, "Oh, I think you can be."

His skepticism hit painfully close to home. "Please go away and leave me alone. I have to get dressed."

"Okay, I will for now, but I don't plan on giving up." He let go of her arm.

She unconsciously rubbed the spot where her skin still tingled from his touch and watched him turn and let himself back into his room, closing the door behind him.

All at once she became aware that the corridor was empty now and quiet. But she still felt uneasy, and it was all to do with Luke.

He'd already shown how persistent he could be. But she had the horrible feeling the reason for that was that he knew exactly what effect he had on her. She headed down the corridor toward her own room, her bare feet sinking into the carpet, pondering how to keep out of his way until she found her quarry.

Damn Luke Dalton. In less than twenty-four hours he'd intruded on her life enough to throw off her concentration when she needed it most. Well, as of this moment she was going to *stop* thinking about him and apply herself to what really mattered—finding James. Because when she did find him, she'd take great pleasure in wringing his neck.

That cheerful prospect almost helped dispel her lingering uneasiness, and the persistent memory of a pair of disturbing ice blue eyes.

As she went into her room a hand grabbed her from behind. Before she could make a sound, another hand clamped over her mouth. Struggling desperately, she tried to wrench away, but the viselike arm pinned her like a steel band.

The door slammed behind her. She wriggled and kicked, but the harder she fought, the tighter the grip. At last she went still, hearing only the harsh sound of her own breathing and the pounding thunder of blood in her ears.

3

"YOU'RE NOT going to scream, are you?"

At the sound of the familiar voice in her ear, her fear dissipated, but all her pent-up frustration exploded in a blaze of anger. She shook her head and the hand was removed from her mouth.

"No, I'm going to kill you!" she shouted as a strong grip turned her around to see that familiar face, the trim mustache and beard, more salt than pepper now.

"Shh, keep your voice down, do you want everyone in the whole bloody hotel to hear you?"

"Don't shush me, you horrible, conniving, dishonest, sneaking thief!" She pushed him away, hard, sending him staggering backward. Planting her hands on her hips, she glared at him.

"Is that any way to talk to your father?" he admonished patiently in the soft Scottish burr that was the only vestige of his Edinburgh childhood.

Stepping closer, he kissed her cheek, a warm, prickly-soft touch against her skin.

"Is this any way to treat your daughter?" But even as she made the accusation she felt relief and thankfulness as she wrapped her arms around him. He felt solid and warm and safe. Safe! Then her anger welled up once more and she pushed him away again. "Do you know what you've put me through over the past couple of days!"

He gave her a bland look. "No, I'm afraid I don't."

Long experience had taught her that she'd get nowhere with James by losing her temper, but she wasn't about to let him off the hook. "You gave me the fright of my life! And you don't even have the grace to be the least bit repentant!"

Far from repentant, he just looked annoyed. "Obviously, Albert's been blabbing. Why doesn't that old fool just mind his own business!"

"Would you keep your voice down! We don't want to attract everybody's attention, remember?" she parroted. "And Albert *is* minding his own business. His business is looking after you."

"What exactly did he tell you?"

"He told me you were coming here to steal a coronet. Looks like you helped yourself to a little more than that," she said caustically. "Now you're going to give back that poor woman's jewelry and come home with me."

"What poor woman's jewelry?" He completely ignored the part about leaving the island, but she wasn't going to let him double-talk his way out of this.

"Are you going to try and deny that you stole Maisie Fleming's diamonds?"

A tight little knot of hurt and betrayal formed in her throat.

"I did not steal her diamonds." There was no passionate denial in his quiet voice, nothing revealed by his closed, almost mulish expression.

She knew that look. No matter what she said, he'd go ahead and do what he wanted. "It's been fourteen years since you retired from all that. You've done so well, don't throw it all away." Her throat tightened and tears clouded her eyes. "Please, Dad."

James's expression softened. He stepped nearer, put his arms around her and pulled her close. She laid her head on his shoulder, comforted for a moment by the familiar scent of him that somehow meant warmth and refuge. She loved him so much, and he was all she had left. If anything should happen to him ... She shuddered, unable to bear the thought of it.

His arms tightened fractionally around her for a moment. "I have no intention of throwing it all away. And I did not steal Maisie What's-her-name's diamonds."

Claire searched his face for the truth. She let out a deep, thankful breath. "If you didn't do it, then who did?"

A slow, grim smile curved his lips beneath the neat gray mustache. In spite of his cavalier attitude, he *did* care what she thought. "I don't know. When did this happen?"

"Last night."

"Damn. This complicates things." He frowned.

"Would you please tell me what the hell is happening? What did Albert mean about you coming here to steal a coronet? What coronet?"

"You obviously only got half the story out of that interfering old gossip."

An unwilling smile came to her lips. He'd be utterly lost without his loyal Albert, who never hesitated to give back as good as he got.

"Abuse him all you like, his opinion of you is equally unflattering. He called you a silly old fool who's going to get himself killed." With malicious amusement she saw his brow crease in annoyance. If there was one thing he hated, it was being called old.

"But that's all beside the point." The knot of fear and worry in her chest had slowly begun to dissipate. His calmness, his very presence, was reassuring. "What *are* you doing here, then?"

"I'd rather not say. I don't want you involved in all this, I just want you to go home."

She walked farther into the sunny room and sat down on the cushioned wicker chair beside the sliding-glass doors. Folding her arms, she gave her father a stubborn look. "I'm not going anywhere until you tell me exactly what you're up to."

He had the nerve to look exasperated. "Kids!"

She glared back at him and held her ground.

At length he sighed and walked over to stand looking down at her, his face grim as he crossed his arms. "It's very important that you go away from here, Claire. We mustn't even be seen together."

"What do you mean? Whyever not?"

"Let's just say it's not a good idea," he said evasively, and moved away to look out the balcony doors.

The relief of finding him was quickly giving way to aggravation. She felt confused and just about at the end of her rope.

Getting to her feet, she moved closer and stopped just behind him. "Why?"

"I think I'm being watched." Claire opened her mouth to speak, but he forestalled her by turning and raising his hand. "I don't know why, or by whom."

A million questions went swirling around her brain. "If you don't know who's watching you, how do you know you're being watched?"

"Instinct."

She snorted unsympathetically. "All the more reason for you to come home with me. Now."

He shook his head and the familiar mulish expression settled on his face. "I can't."

"You are."

He shook his head again and her heart sank at the stubborn set of his firm mouth. "I can't leave this island till I've done what I came to do."

She knew that unyielding tone all too well. "I'm not in the mood for your tricks. All this 'a man's got to do what a man's got to do' nonsense doesn't wash with me."

A knock at the door startled her, setting her heart pounding with fear. James swiftly put a finger to his lips and indicated she should stay still. Then sanity asserted itself. What was the matter with her? All this cloak-and-dagger nonsense was turning her into a nervous wreck!

"It's probably just the..." With a sharp gesture, James motioned her to be quiet. "It's probably just the maid," she finished in a whisper.

"Whoever it is, get rid of them. Don't let them in," he said softly, then went to stand behind the door.

Annoyed at his ridiculous behavior, and feeling more than a little foolish, she went to answer the knock.

Luke stood in the corridor. His straight mouth curved in that wolfish smile and his eyes gleamed dangerously as he looked down at her.

"Will you come and have breakfast with me?" He came right to the point, his voice as deep, soft and dark as black velvet.

She looked up and a small shiver of apprehension went through her. "No."

"Please?"

She darted a glance at James on the other side of the door and noticed distractedly that the two men were exactly the same height. Her father was rolling his eyes heavenward in derision.

"I can't," she said, fighting the annoyance James could so easily provoke.

Somehow she still hoped to persuade her father to leave, so she might not even be on the island an hour from now. But to her surprise the prospect suddenly filled her with wistful regret.

"You know, Claire...I just want to get to know you, nothing more."

His deep voice was so sincere. But then he'd sounded equally sincere when he'd returned her filched passport, she reminded herself ruthlessly.

And yet she couldn't deny her desire to get to know much more about him, too. And not just because his proximity set this strange new hunger burning inside her.

"So how about it?" he prompted.

She shook her head. "I'm sorry. That's impossible."

"Impossible? Nothing's impossible," he coaxed.

Oh, how she wanted to say yes. But she *couldn't*. He said he didn't want more, but she *did*. That was what terrified her, and he knew it, too.

From the corner of her eye she caught James's disgusted glare.

"I have to go." *I have to go and wipe that smug, judgmental look off my father's face.*

She went to close the door, but instead of stepping back Luke reached out and gently trailed his fingers down her cheek. Claire stifled a little intake of breath at the explicit rush of tingling heat.

"Claire," he murmured, the one word darkly seductive.

"No, I can't." She resisted the urge to say yes. "Now, please, go away and leave me alone."

He gave her a long, unsmiling look and let out a small sigh. "Okay. But never have I admitted defeat so unwillingly." Then turned and walked away.

As she closed the door she felt proud of herself for not giving in to temptation. Spending time with him would be crazy. The way he made her feel was a needless complication. At the sound of James's chuckling, she turned to face him with annoyance.

"I wonder how many poor fools fall for that line, 'I just want to get to know you.'" James chortled again.

Bristling, she immediately jumped to Luke's defense. "Don't make fun of him! You don't even know him. He happens to be a very nice man."

"Very nice man, my arse. He's just another two-bit Romeo looking for a good time. And if you fall for that line of his, my girl, you've got no more brains than those simpering twits who come here looking for that sort of thing." His soft burr vibrated with disdainful amusement.

"What do you know? You don't even know him."

"What's his name?" he asked laconically.

"Luke Dalton."

"Where's he from?"

"I don't know."

He cocked a bristling eyebrow. "What does he do for a living?"

"I don't know." In dismay she felt the ground slipping from beneath her.

"And *I* don't know him?" James chuckled and she felt her hands curling up into tight balls. "Seems to me *you're* the one who doesn't know him."

What could she say? To her chagrin there was no denying the cold, hard truth. She *wanted* to see Luke. She *wanted* to explore the fantasy. But she certainly didn't want to discuss it with her father right now. Besides, she'd already told Luke she wasn't interested, so there was really nothing to discuss. The thought left her depressed.

"Anyway, we're not talking about me," she said more sharply than necessary. "We're talking about you now, so quit trying to change the subject and start talking."

James pinned her with a keen, thoughtful look. She couldn't hide a damn thing from her father.

"Well..." she prompted. "What are you waiting for?"

He heaved an exaggerated sigh of impatience, then moved to the couch and sat down. Leaning back, he stretched out his long legs in sand-colored linen trousers, and carefully regarded his rope-soled canvas shoes. "First of all, I have no intention of resuming my former career. That was over and done with a long time ago."

Her shoulders sagged in relief. "Then what are you doing here?"

"Let me start from the beginning."

"Please do." She tried to curb her sarcasm and walked over to sink into the armchair near him.

"Three weeks ago Karl Battenburg came to see me." He paused thoughtfully. "You've heard of the coronet of Wittgenstein?"

The name triggered a memory. "The eight-pointed crown of fleur-de-lis and Maltese crosses?"

"That's the one, very good."

His nod of approval took her right back to when she was seventeen and James would quiz her on the glittering contents of the Bulgari Jewelers' display window.

Name the cut, estimate how many carats... was that mounting, silver or platinum? He was always testing her knowledge.

Other than now, that had been the only time his former profession had made an impact on her life, leading directly to her present career with one of the most prestigious auction houses in Toronto. At thirty, she was their youngest expert and she owed that to his early tutelage. Her father had passed on his fascination with precious stones and fine jewelry. Unlike her father, however, she had confined her fascination to the straight and narrow.

"I saw the coronet a couple of years ago. It was on display briefly at the van Beuningen museum in Rotterdam. It was simply incredible."

Who could forget that amazing crown in its glass case, set on a bed of royal blue velvet? Each point was surmounted with pear-shaped pearls the size of robins' eggs, and encrusted with countless smaller stones. But what made the crown even more remarkable were the heart-shaped Navarre diamonds, each over fifty carats, set into the fleur-de-lis, and the magnificent twenty-five-carat, table-cut Star of Siam in the center cross.

"Well, it was stolen," James said bluntly. "And it's somewhere in this hotel."

Claire gave a low whistle, then shook her head, confused again. "But what does that have to do with Karl?"

"Everything. It belongs to him."

Claire could only gape in amazement, remembering the courtly little old man who'd come to visit on several occasions while she'd been living with her father.

"The crown jewels of the principality of Wittgenstein belong to Karl Battenburg?"

"Yes. His title is Prince Ottolon of Wittgenstein. Of course you know the country was swallowed up by the Soviet Union after the war."

Karl's exalted origins had never been mentioned, and she'd never guessed. But now, thinking back, she could see the products of that aristocratic birthright in his Old World grace and charm.

"So, anyway, he came to see you..." she prompted.

"Yes. Needless to say, he was devastated by the theft. It was all he had left."

"When did this happen, and how?"

"Three weeks ago. A professional job commissioned by a wealthy collector who lives somewhere in the Caribbean. The coronet is now in the possession of a courier hired to deliver it to him. The courier is somewhere on this island and I have to find him before he delivers his 'cargo.'"

She expelled her breath in dismay. "It would be worth... well, it's priceless. The historical significance alone..."

"Exactly."

"But what does it have to do with you? Why didn't he go to the police?"

"He did. But he knows as well as I do that the police are too busy. And it wasn't even insured."

She groaned softly. "Well, that takes care of my next question. Insurance investigators would be relentless in tracking down something that valuable."

"Yes, but the premiums would have been astronomical. Karl couldn't afford the insurance."

She felt a pang of pity for the old man. "Yes, but I repeat, what has it got to do with you?"

Her father gave a dry chuckle. "It takes a thief to catch a thief."

"Oh, no, you don't." A cold shudder went down her spine. She stood abruptly and began to pace the floor in front of him, twisting her hands together.

"Claire, it's his only chance." His voice was quietly decisive. "If it helps, don't think of it as stealing, think of it as restoring something to its rightful owner."

"Look, nothing you say will convince me . . ."

"I'm not trying to convince you, just trying to explain why I'm doing it."

"But you can't." She stopped pacing to plead directly. "Think of the dangers, think of the risks."

"Claire, without me, he has no hope of recovering it."

She dropped down on the sofa beside him, beset by a terrible premonition that something was going to happen to him. The thought made her feel helpless and frightened.

"It's too risky," she said in a throaty whisper.

"Some things are worth the risk. This crown is important."

"Why?" she said in frustration, and flopped back against the cushions, folding her arms. "So the prince can gaze at it and remember former glories?"

At this moment she didn't feel the least bit charitable toward a man who was putting her father in such an awkward, not to mention, dangerous, position.

"No, for the people of Wittgenstein." It was a patient, quiet reproof. "They've just regained independence after all these years of communist rule and he was intending to donate the crown to the people."

"Oh." She shifted restlessly, feeling ashamed of her quickness to judge. "But why you? Worthy cause or not, your safety is still at risk, and you can't expect me not to worry."

"I owe him my life," he said simply. "If it hadn't been for Karl, my mother and sisters and I would never have made it out of Europe when the war started. We'd probably have been thrown into an internment camp."

She knew the story of how, as a boy of ten, he and his family had been hidden and smuggled out of occupied France on a fishing boat. She could understand his gratitude.

"But it's been years since you did anything like this," she objected. "You're not exactly a young man anymore."

"Well, I'm hardly old."

In spite of the fear churning in her stomach, James's bristling indignation brought a wry smile to her lips.

"No, but you're not up to the physical dangers." She took perverse pleasure in needling him. He deserved it.

"You have a lot of faith, don't you?" He was put out, his male pride wounded.

"It's got nothing to do with faith. Who do you think you're up against here? Some poor unsuspecting victim? There's no such thing as a gentleman thief anymore. This guy is a pro. Nowadays, thieves don't just steal, they kill people to do it. And I'd rather turn you in to the police myself, than see you dead!"

"Then you'll have to turn me in, because I've made up my mind. I'm going to do this. I have to do this." There was no mistaking the steely determination in his voice, in the tight, firm lips and hard-set jaw under the neatly barbered beard. Then he softened a little. "Don't worry about me, Claire. I promise I won't get myself injured, killed, or arrested. Now be a good girl and go home."

"No, I'm staying right here," she said calmly. "And if you're going to go ahead with this ridiculous, childish scheme, then I'm going to help you."

"What!" He was on his feet and halfway across the room in long, angry strides before turning to face her. "No way!"

"You either quit and come home with me, or I'm going to stay and help you."

He walked purposefully toward her, one finger held up sternly. "Claire Elizabeth Sterling, you listen to me..."

She knew that tone of voice. That "father" tone that invariably told her he meant business, but this time she ignored it. She got to her feet, ready to do battle. "No, you listen to me. If you persist in this reckless and irresponsible..."

"Irresponsible!" he said, glaring down at her.

"Irresponsible venture," she continued firmly, "then I am going to help. *Comprende*?"

After a few moments, his brooding face filled with exasperation and he sighed. "Why do you have to be so stubborn?"

"Why do you?"

For a long moment they stared each other down. Then all at once something warm stole into his eyes and, with a feeling of relief, Claire knew she'd won, for now anyway.

She stepped closer, put her arms around his neck and, going up a little on tiptoe, kissed the end of his nose.

His arms came around her and he said with gruff fondness, "You're a bloody nuisance, do you know that?"

"Yes, I know." She grinned at him and he smiled unwillingly back.

"All right, you can help." Grudgingly he gave in, but then his expression hardened and he lifted a warning finger in front of her face. "*But*, you do exactly what I tell you, *when* I tell you."

She heaved a sigh of her own. It was a questionable victory.

"Have you got that straight?" he demanded.

"Yes, and you don't have to shout." She stepped away from him and walked over to the sliding doors, squinting against the glare of the morning sun. "So what do I do first?"

His reply was concise and uncompromising. "Stay out of my way."

She spun around. "Now wait a minute. That's *not* what I meant by helping. And don't think you can fob me off."

He gave another long-suffering sigh. "I wish I could. But you can't do anything until I've found the courier. And I don't even know who he is yet. All I have is a general description of the man. A few clues." He began pacing slowly. Stroking his beard, deep in thought, he said, more to himself than her, "I hope I can find him before the competition does."

"Speaking of the competition, I saw him last night on the Flemings' balcony. I thought it was you."

He looked up sharply, his interest piqued. "Did you notice anything about him, anything identifiable?"

Claire shook her head. "No."

"Damn," he swore under his breath.

"Well, give me a break. It was dark, he was dressed in black from head to foot. What was I supposed to notice? As it is, I almost killed myself trying to get to him."

His eyes narrowed. "What do you mean?"

"Balcony hopping isn't exactly my forte," she said sarcastically, feeling nettled. Could he have done any better?

"You risked your life hopping balconies!" He looked aghast and disgusted. "That was bloody stupid, wasn't it? What were you planning to do when you caught up with him?"

"I was planning on wringing his neck because I thought it was you!" she ground out through clenched teeth. Obviously a pat on the back for her bravery was the last thing she could expect.

For a long moment he stared at her in exasperation, then his expression softened. "You'd risk your life for me?"

"Of course I'd risk my life for you!" she exploded. "I love you, you idiot!"

Her fury brought a smile to his lips. "Careful, you're starting to sound like me."

He was impossible. "So what do I do in the meantime to help?"

"Do?" He seemed to think it an asinine question. "Enjoy your holiday, what else? Go sight-seeing. Do the things other tourists do. Blend in. And remember..." He walked over to stand in front of her. Once more he raised his finger and his voice became forbidding as he emphasized every word, *"You don't know me."*

"Isn't that being a little melodramatic..."

"If you're not going to take this seriously you can go home right now."

"Okay, okay." She held up her hands in surrender. "I don't know you."

"Good. One last thing."

"What?"

A small smile appeared in his dark eyes. "I love you."

Then he put his arms around her and hugged her close, kissing her cheek.

She hugged him back fiercely, terrifyingly aware of how safe and secure this felt, and how easily she could lose him. "I love you, too."

"Don't worry," he admonished gruffly. "I won't get myself killed. Have some faith in your dad." Then he gently disengaged himself. "I'll be in touch."

In a moment he was at the door, listening, then he opened it a crack to take a cautious look. A second later he slipped out, with a quick backward glance that silently reminded her to stay calm and do as she was told.

Claire wrapped her arms tightly around herself, suddenly overcome by a surge of pure, unadulterated fear. *Please, let him be all right*, she prayed.

A light knock sounded at the door. What did he forget? She moved quickly to open it. The heady lure of danger fizzed through her veins like champagne, and once again she felt a wave of heightened excitement that set her blood pounding in her ears.

His voice reached out to caress her—husky and intimate. "I'm going to give you one more chance . . ."

4

"OH YOU ARE, are you?" Claire felt a reckless thrill. "I'm *so* grateful."

"You should be, I'm not usually so persistent." He mimicked her sarcasm, then his smile became rueful. And those eyes, how they held hers—simmering with sensuality. But suddenly there was a touch of uncertainty there that made him completely irresistible.

"So what's different this time?"

"You," he said softly as his hungry gaze burned a slow path over her face, as if he were committing her to memory. No man had ever looked at her like that before. It made her feel breathless.

Steady on Claire. This was all just a game; he was flirting and she wasn't meant to take any of it seriously. The trouble was, he made her feel sensations she never knew existed.

Suddenly she wanted to explore this vibrant, stimulating new feeling. Was there any harm in a little flirtation? How much trouble could she get into in such a short time?

James's words rang in her ears. *Enjoy your holiday...* Why not?

She finally answered in a slow, sarcastic drawl. "Little old me? Well...you quite take my breath away." Yet she said it with a smile meant to clearly convey that she wasn't repulsing him.

"Does that mean you'll come with me?" His dark gaze brushed over her like tantalizing fingertips.

"Come with you?" She still sensed danger. "Where?"

"To St. Vincent." His voice vibrated with the low purr of a jungle cat.

"What's in St. Vincent?" *Who cared?*

"Adventure."

A hot current of sexuality burned the air between them, a million-volt charge sizzling across that two feet of space.

"What kind of adventure?"

Luke could see the excitement in her glowing eyes, hear it in the subtle deepening of her voice.

Was that why she stole, for the kick? For the sheer adventure and challenge? It couldn't be for the money. She would inherit a tidy estate from her father, and besides that, in her own work she was well-paid and well-respected. Very impressive for only thirty. The woman had that lethal combination—brains and beauty. That's why he had to watch his step.

But now at least he knew how to hook her interest.

"That's the whole point of having an adventure," he said. "It's the element of surprise. If I tell you, it'll take away half the fun."

It could be just as much of an adventure staying here and finding out where all that sexual awareness could lead, but that would be asking for trouble. And he'd get it, in spades.

Still, it was impossible to ignore the knowledge that he only had to make one small move and they could end up spending the day in her bed.

"How do I know I can trust you? I don't know you."

She couldn't. He took a deep breath and tried very hard not to think of her lying on the bed, looking up at him with that little smile of hers, so innocent, so provocative... so maddening. No, she couldn't trust him. Not as far as she could throw him.

"I suppose you have to let your instinct guide you." It took an effort to dredge up an appropriately earnest expression. "Do you trust me, Claire?"

In amazement he saw her cheeks go pink before she dropped her gaze and turned away from him.

Impatient with himself, he knew he should feel satisfied, but all he could feel was tension building—and guilt. Why should he feel guilty? Had he forgotten so soon what she'd been doing on his balcony last night? And then this morning, to have the gall to go and commiserate with her victim!

"So what do you think, Claire?"

"But what if it's something I wouldn't enjoy?"

"Oh, you'll enjoy it." With ruthless deliberation, he made his voice alluring and seductive, gave it that ring of mystery guaranteed to reel her in. "I give you my solemn promise."

He'd been acting out of character ever since Claire Sterling came on the scene. No, even before that. He'd been concerned he was losing his edge. Perhaps he was getting too old for this business. Leave it to the younger guys with nerves of steel.

Normally he wouldn't have these qualms. You did what you had to do to get the job done. And what he had to do was keep an eye on her. His mouth twisted with bitter irony. She could actually be useful to him today.

"I suppose that's meant to reassure me? The word of a man who admitted to stealing my passport." Her voice was a little husky but she had regained her composure.

At any other time he would admire her tenacity, her courage. But not now. "Is it my fault that you can drive a man to such desperate measures? What do you say, yes or no?"

His voice teased her, but those eyes held something darker. Clear, crystal blue, they challenged her, compelled her, burned with a cold, hungry fire. She couldn't go on with this banter a second longer.

Besides, she didn't want to resist anymore. She wanted to go with him, to find out for herself what his eyes were promising.

"Oh, why not."

Something hard and ruthless tightened his face even as he smiled. "Great."

The way he said that one word made her think for a moment that her answer didn't please him. She felt confused and unsure.

Then his smile broadened and that brief, pitiless shadow vanished. "Then why are we standing here? Go get ready."

After three days of anxiety and paranoia, perhaps her imagination was still playing tricks on her. And besides, this man was such an enigma she was probably misreading him.

That was undoubtedly part of the reason she wanted to go—to get to know him. And hadn't James told her to stay out of his way?

"What do I need to bring?"

"Just a bathing suit." Luke gave her a slow smile that made her shiver with excitement.

Perhaps this *was* all a strange dream. In the past forty-eight hours she'd gone from being a level-headed, responsible person to an oversexed, paranoid, yet incredibly reckless, would-be thief. And it wasn't over yet.

But one thing she knew for sure, if she didn't go with Luke Dalton today, she'd regret it for the rest of her life.

THE HELICOPTER shuttle put them down on the edge of Kingstown, the capital of the lush volcanic island of St. Vincent. A small van took them into town.

They spent the morning exploring the pretty little town beside the bay, nestled below slopes of emerald green tropical forest.

There was nothing of the stranger, or the tourist about Luke as he took her through the sun-washed streets of low buildings, exploring the shops tucked beneath arched arcades that provided shelter from the blazing sun.

In the taxi ride up to British Fort Charlotte, dominating the town from a rocky bluff, he told her about the part it played in repelling French attempts to capture the island.

"But you know it's not just a museum," he said as they strolled across the open courtyard. "It's gruesome past isn't so long ago."

"What do you mean?"

"They still hold public hangings here." Stopping beside the stone walls, he looked down on the town below.

Claire leaned her arms on the rough stone. "You're joking."

"No, I'm not."

"Sounds positively medieval." She laughed, still not quite taking him seriously. "What do you mean, like bring the kids, make a day of it? Do they charge you admission?"

"No, seriously." There was no answering smile on his face. "The last hanging took place in 1979. A father and son."

"Uh-oh, a family affair," she said lightly but shivered in the noonday sun.

"I suppose it pays to be on the right side of the law."

She didn't feel like joining in his casual laughter. Theft might not be a hanging offense any longer, but the consequences of being caught didn't bear thinking of. She tried to push it out of her mind.

From the spectacular vantage point of the fort, Luke pointed out the hazy shapes of the Grenadine islands, strung out like green jewels on the horizon. But Claire couldn't shake the morbid shadow his story had left behind. It was a grim reminder of which side of the law she was operating on right now, and she was glad when they left the fort.

She distracted herself by asking questions about his background. Luke told a few amusing family anecdotes, but somehow he always deftly turned her questions around and she found herself talking about *her* life.

His sincere interest was flattering. And always, that warm appreciation simmered deep down in his eyes. He was the perfect companion, showing her a wonderful time, and she was becoming more and more fascinated with him by the moment.

He must have read that fascination on her face, but to her surprise he did nothing to take advantage of it. When he did touch her it was only a casual cupping of her elbow or a light hand on her back. Yet that contact was enough to make her skin warm and tingly.

For lunch he took her to a café down by the harbor. In the shade of a striped awning, she watched the yachts and sailboats plying the blue waters and relished her delicious meal of red snapper. As they finished their coffee, Luke suggested they spend the afternoon snorkeling.

"But I don't know how to snorkel," she protested. Yet somehow she felt no anxiety.

At this point she was ready to go along with anything he might suggest. After the way they'd met, it seemed unbelievable that she could now feel so content and carefree.

"There's nothing to it," he assured her. "I'll show you, don't worry."

"You make it sound so easy." She smiled.

"It is, like falling off a log." He smiled back, his eyes crinkling at the corners with a warm reassurance that turned her fascination into heady excitement.

For this stolen day she wanted to forget her worries—about James, about everything. And she refused to waste one moment feeling guilty and irresponsible. She would have to go back and face things anyway, but for now she was determined to damn well enjoy this day!

When they left the restaurant Luke led her down the wooden steps to the wharf and headed toward the farthest end where small fishing boats were tied up.

Gulls cried and wheeled overhead and the air was filled with the overpowering smell of fish. Skinny, ragged children darted and played between the men mending their nets. Claire noticed the way they looked up in silent curiosity at Luke.

And why not? There was something vital and commanding about the economical grace of his movements, so smooth and self-assured. With the sun glinting on his dark hair as he strolled down the concrete pier, he looked as relaxed as if he were in his own backyard.

And yet he radiated that keen alertness. Once she'd found it sinister, but now it was only one stimulating facet of a very exciting package.

Nearing the end of the pier, they stopped beside a small, slightly shabby-looking boat with the name *Golden Lady* painted on the bow in faded lettering. At that moment a tall, stocky black man emerged from the cabin.

Luke greeted the man warmly. "Claire, I'd like you to meet Samuel Bonaire. Sam, this is Claire Sterling."

She nodded and smiled uncertainly, but no answering smile appeared on the man's face. Samuel looked at her, silent and faintly disapproving. Then his gaze slid to Luke in an unspoken inquiry.

But Luke just smiled and patted his massive shoulder as he stepped down into the boat. He held out his hand to her.

"Come on, we don't have all day," he teased but his voice held amusement and intimacy.

As she stepped into the bobbing boat the motion sent her lurching against him. His arms immediately went around her to steady her, pulling her body close. The heady, masculine scent of him filled her senses and she felt him against her, warm and hard.

"Where are we going?" she asked breathlessly.

"I told you, on an adventure," he murmured. His suddenly hot gaze rested on her parted lips before coming back to the throbbing awareness he must see in her eyes.

"Oh." Shakily she pushed away from his unresisting arms and turned to find Samuel watching them, his expression inscrutable.

On unsteady legs she made her way to the front of the boat. She couldn't face Luke till she had herself under control. Leaning against the side, she watched but didn't really pay attention to Samuel making preparations to cast off.

"Just 'oh'?" Luke sounded amused.

He'd come to lean on the rail beside her, but instead of watching Samuel his attention was focused on her.

His voice became quiet and serious. "Do you trust me that much that you would go with me and not insist on an explanation?"

She turned and met his eyes with a level, unwavering look. For once it was a relief to be honest. "I suppose I must."

There was something about him, in spite of everything that had happened, that made her feel safe. Was it just that aura of competence about him, that strength and vitality?

"What if I told you I was taking you to a private island retreat and keeping you there as my love slave?"

"Are you?"

"No. But it sounds good, doesn't it?" He grinned, his eyes glinting with mischief.

"Not the slave part, thank you," she said tartly, and gave him a look to match.

But the thought of being alone with him, doing whatever he wanted of her, forced into pleasuring him... A deep shudder tore through her.

Luke chuckled low in his throat. "Okay, how about if we change that to—I take you to a private island and *I'll* be your love slave?"

Just the thought sent her imagination into overdrive again. Heat suffused her body, her flushed face betrayed her.

"Now that sounds more like it."

She tried to make it sound like offhand banter, but she was terrified to look up at him. He was too perceptive, how could he not have guessed her thoughts?

And then his voice was suddenly close behind her, his warm breath tickling her ear. "We don't need the private island, but I'll be your slave, if you want me."

His voice was low and vibrant with suppressed laughter. Of course he was joking. If he were serious, she'd be in big trouble. She was too weak to say no.

If she'd come for a Caribbean holiday, looking for the ultimate fantasy, she'd feel her money had been well-spent.

All the elements were here—the lush, tropical island paradise of swaying palms and soft sands, the cloudless blue sky above and the turquoise waters below as the boat headed out of the bay. But most of all the man beside her—darkly handsome, beguiling and mysterious. A woman would have to be made of stone not to melt at that irresistible offer.

Was that the lure for him, too? Did he come to these islands to live the fantasy himself?

With herculean effort she forced her voice to sound offhand. "All right, you can be my slave, and you can start by getting me something cold to drink."

He remained perfectly still and she forced herself to turn to look up into his eyes.

There was no smile in his eyes. They met hers with assessing acuity, as if searching her face for the truth, then the corners of his mouth curved in a slow, lazy grin and he bowed his head. "Your wish is my command."

He moved away toward the stern and disappeared around the other side of the wheelhouse.

With any other man she could easily play the flirtation game and hold her own.

The trouble was that, away from him, she was intrigued and tantalized, wanting to know more about him. But when she was with him... she felt vulnerable and scared and every tiny part of her seemed to vibrate with this low, humming excitement, this conviction that something momentous was going to happen. The thought raised little goose bumps on her skin. She hugged herself and rubbed her bare arms.

She glanced up to the wheelhouse to see Samuel standing with one hand on the wheel, watching her with that stolid suspicion that made her uneasy. After all, here she was, on the open sea in a small boat with one complete stranger and a man who was still a disturbing enigma to her.

She turned away from Samuel's probing eyes and sat down on a pile of coiled ropes.

A few moments later Luke sat beside her, not touching but close enough to make her pulse throb as he handed her an ice-cold can of pop.

Taking it from him, her fingers brushed his, sending a tremor racing up her arm. She looked quickly up at him to see if he'd noticed her involuntary reaction, but he was looking out to sea, his eyes squinting against the glare so that she couldn't read his expression.

"Look! Over there."

And she was glad to look, anywhere but at him.

He pointed toward a small school of dolphins leaping and flashing through the water.

As they got farther away from St. Vincent the massive peak of Mount Soufrière became visible at the northern end of the island, veiled behind a ring of smoky cloud. Although it looked serene, Luke told her that the last major eruption had been as recent as 1979.

But even as she focused on the sights and tried to pay attention to what he was saying, every part of her was electrically aware of him.

Everything shimmered in the pure, clear light. Below them the water was incredibly translucent, so that the boat seemed to skim suspended above the ocean floor so far below. She was hopelessly out of her depth, and more than a little panicked.

The stiff breeze tore loose a lock of hair from her ponytail and she nervously tucked it behind her ear. Hadn't she thrown caution to the winds and come along? So why shouldn't she just relax and enjoy it? Nothing would happen unless she wanted it to.

"So, where *are* we going?" Turning to face him, she nestled against the curve of the rail, pulled a strand of hair away from her eyes and smiled up at him.

"Just a little south of here, off a tiny atoll the locals call Blood Island."

"Sounds like a charming place," she said drolly.

"Oh, it is. Especially in the old days, when the evil pirate Percy—"

"Percy the Pirate?" She chuckled.

"Ah, now that's just it. Anyone caught making fun of his name in any way was brought to this island and left to die. Very sensitive about his name, was old Percy." A mischievous smile curved his lips, causing two small dimples to appear.

Her heart did a funny little flip-flop and she laughed breathlessly. "I can understand why."

"They say his ghost ship haunts the reef, so not many people come here. That's one of the reasons I do. It's very private. That way I can pretend I'm Pirate Percy and lure some poor wench to satisfy my wicked desires." He waggled his dark brows with an insinuating, suggestive leer that made her laugh.

"And no doubt you've brought many an unsuspecting victim here before me."

Suddenly there was something very serious in his eyes. "Now what makes you think I'm joking? I could have evil designs on you. And there's nobody here to help."

She shook her head slowly and responded with equal seriousness. "I know I can trust you."

"How do you know that? You hardly know anything about me," he said quietly.

"I can sense it."

For a brief moment he turned away, squinting out across the water. Then he returned his gaze to her, and smiled a slow, wry smile.

"You poor fool, that's how I lure them all to their doom." He leaned forward, waggling his eyebrows again with that comically lecherous grin, all signs of the darkness she had glimpsed so briefly, gone.

She decided to take her cue from him and keep her tone light. "You might very well be luring me to my doom. I told you, I've never snorkeled before."

He sat back, leaning against the wooden boards with one arm draped over the stern rail.

"Don't worry, I'll take good care of you. All jokes aside, I'm glad you realize you don't have to be afraid of being alone with me. I wouldn't hurt you." There was something dark and brooding and very serious in his eyes.

She took a deep breath and shakily let it out. "What makes you think that it's *you* I'm afraid of?"

5

"I'M FLATTERED." His voice was warm but guarded. "And you *still* have nothing to worry about," he said with a smile, the wind ruffling his dark hair.

But he was wrong. She had plenty to worry about. She was slipping painlessly into what James would scathingly call "Phase One." But how could she help it? He was only the most exciting, most potently masculine man she'd ever met.

And that was the part that baffled her. He wasn't her usual type at all. He was too aggressive. He had the air of a man used to giving orders and having them obeyed.

But this time was going to be different. This time she wasn't going to get all tangled up in knots. Even *she* couldn't get too involved in the space of a few days. So why *not* just enjoy the experience?

A few minutes later Luke pointed to a shimmering green dot on the starboard side. "There it is, Blood Island."

Samuel steered the boat toward the small atoll. He cut the engine a few hundred yards from shore. Here they were, all alone.

Ahead lay a dreamy paradise isle of swaying palms, white sand and the lush, vibrant green of tropical foliage. The scent of flowers came wafting toward her over the water and she could only shake her head. "No island could have been more misnamed. It's so beautiful."

"Yes, very," he murmured softly, a slight edge to his voice.

She looked up to find Luke watching her, something grim in his expression. Then it was gone and he gave her a small, lazy smile.

"You can go down below to change into your bathing suit."

She sighed inwardly. Along with being the most exciting man she'd ever met, he was also the most confusing. Picking up her bag, she went around to the back of the wheelhouse. Hurrying down the steps, she went through a low doorway into a small, neatly fitted cabin with a narrow bunk and tiny galley at one end.

As she slipped into her maillot she prayed she wouldn't make too much of a fool of herself over this man. She shrugged off the thought. So what? After the next couple of days, she'd never see him again anyway.

But coming back up the steps her breath suddenly caught in her throat at the sight of Luke standing on deck ahead of her, tall, lean, and utterly arresting in black swim trunks.

He was putting on his flippers with focused concentration, everything about him clean and chiseled in the pure, clear light—the firm line of his jaw, the hard, sculpted contours of his bare, tanned chest. But it wasn't just good looks that almost stopped her in her tracks. It was the power and purpose in every line of his body, the uncompromising masculinity.

He looked up and saw her, and his face softened in a smile. "Come on up here and I'll show you how to put all this stuff on."

She walked toward him, feeling shy. "It all looks so complicated," she said for want of something—anything—to say.

"Looks can be deceiving." Although his eyes crinkled in a grin, she thought there was a trace of bitterness there, but it vanished so quickly she dismissed it as imagination.

He helped her with her own pair of long, unwieldy flippers, then quickly and expertly slipped on the rest of his equipment.

She watched Luke strap on a nylon webbing belt and check that a lethal-looking knife was securely in the scabbard resting against his hip.

"What's that for?" she asked anxiously.

"For emergencies. Generally speaking they don't arise."

He was so calm, so matter-of-fact, but immediately she saw images in lurid Technicolor. "Wait a minute, 'emergencies'? You mean like—sharks, giant octopus... man-eating clams!"

He touched her arm. "Relax."

Relax? Fat chance of that. First he'd have to stop touching her arm.

"Are you ready to go on?" He grinned.

"Yes." That grin should be labeled a deadly weapon and banned. He just had to flash it once and she was lost.

He handed her the mask and showed her how to put it on. When the mask covered her face she stiffened, panicked by a moment of claustrophobia, and pushed it up onto her head, taking a deep breath. "I don't know if I can handle this for very long."

"It's all right. Just slip the mouthpiece between your teeth and breathe naturally. You'll get the hang of it. Like this." He demonstrated.

She eyed him dubiously but did as he did. It wasn't so bad once you got used to it.

"Are you all right?"

She nodded.

"Atta girl."

The very real admiration in his eyes had her fears melting away. In spite of her reservations, she'd never been so excited and stimulated before.

He held out his hand. "Let's go see if we can find old Percy's ship."

At that moment Samuel silently materialized beside them and handed Luke a zippered rubber pouch. A silent look passed between the two men and Luke gave him a small, grim nod as he snapped the pouch onto his belt.

Samuel had already hooked a ladder onto the side of the boat and Luke used it to climb over the side and drop lightly into the clear blue water. Feeling awkward in the huge flippers, she cautiously followed. Would she follow him if he jumped off a cliff? Probably, she thought with a wry grimace.

The water was blissfully cool and she felt buoyant and weightless as Luke showed her how to paddle along the surface of the water, looking down through the plastic mask.

Suspended in a blue world, below her lay a living carpet of color and movement.

In only a few moments she got the hang of breathing through the snorkel and discovered that Luke was absolutely right. This was quite easy.

She glanced over at him and he gave her the thumbs up sign. A warm glow spread through her that made the whole undersea paradise beneath her even more spectacular.

Clouds of silver, blue and gold fish darted about, while spiny lobsters and hermit crabs scuttled among coral of fantastically varied shapes and colors.

Wherever she turned she was amazed at all the different kinds of fish. Red and yellow snapper, parrot fish and a hundred other species she'd never seen before.

With Luke beside her she found herself actually relaxing and able to drink in the experience of this fabulous world. It made her realize even more how much she trusted this man, how she sensed that he could handle any situation in the same calm, efficient manner. He made her feel safe.

A small warning bell sounded. With a stab of apprehension, she realized she'd entered another dimension, and she wasn't just thinking of the sea.

He touched her arm and pointed to where the sea floor sloped precipitously another twenty feet or so. At the bottom lay the unmistakable outline of a sunken wreck.

In the clear water she could see that no trace of wood was left, but the coral-encrusted outline of the ribs told the story of a long-ago shipwreck. She smiled, thinking of Luke's highly dubious story of Pirate Percy.

All too soon it seemed, Luke touched her shoulder to get her attention and lifted his head up, treading water. She broke the surface and came up beside him.

Pulling out his mouthpiece, he grinned at her, his dark hair streaming with water. "If you're not too tired, we could swim to the island and go exploring."

"I'm not tired at all." On the contrary, she felt exhilarated. Luke had this effect on her, every minute she was with him.

"Good. Let's go, then."

He replaced his snorkel and struck out for shore. She followed and in a very few minutes felt firm ground under her.

In the waist-high water, Luke emerged beside her and pulled off his snorkel and mask. Tucking them under his arm, he turned to grin at her, his wet hair clinging to his head as droplets of water trickled down his face. She wanted to reach out and smooth them away, drink them from his lips.

But she didn't have the nerve. She just followed his lead, removing her own mask, and soon they were wading up onto a warm sandy beach the color of cream. Reaching the fringe of palm trees, she dropped her gear on the sand and collapsed to her knees in the shade.

Luke sank down beside her as she was pulling off her flippers. She saw his gaze run quickly over her as he did the same. His eyes darkened with a brief flair of desire, quickly reined in as he turned his attention to the sparkling sea. She felt a twinge of disappointment.

Shielding her eyes against the sun, she noticed for the first time that the boat was nowhere in sight.

"Where's Samuel?" After Luke's story of people being abandoned on this island to die, she felt a little alarmed, especially after Samuel's silent hostility.

"He's gone off to do a little fishing. He'll be back," Luke said casually.

If he wasn't worried, then she wouldn't, either. But now they were virtually alone in this incredibly romantic spot. Nothing but sand and sea, the scent of flowers drugging her, and Luke beside her, the most potent drug of all. Painful awareness prickled over her skin. Would he try to make love to her?

"What would you like to do now?" She kept her eyes fixed on a point far out to sea. It was as far as she could bring herself to prompt him.

"Explore the island, of course."

That was not the answer she wanted to hear. He stood with the lithe economical grace that characterized all his movements. He held out a hand to her. "Come on, let's go see what's on the other side. Maybe we'll find one of Percy's victims."

"Now there's an offer I can't refuse." She put her hand in his and let him pull her upright. The tingling went straight up her arm and down to every nerve end.

He grinned at her dry response, but to her intense disappointment he let go of her hand as soon as she was on her feet. With his hands on his hips, he looked past her and surveyed the cloak of green trees rising from the beach.

"What luck, looks like we have a trail over here." He pointed to a spot where the undergrowth was sparse, sounding pleased, like a small boy playing pirates and buried treasure. His enthusiasm was touching and she couldn't help but smile.

"Then, by all means, let's see where it leads to."

Leaving their gear under the palm tree, they followed a path that led steeply uphill. It ended at a shaded grassy knoll overlooking the bay on the other side of the island. A gleaming white yacht stood anchored a short distance offshore.

"Looks like we've got company," Luke said, dropping to his knees. Then he reached up and caught her fingers in a firm grip, pulling her down beside him. Another little tingle raced up her arm as she sat on the coarse grass.

"This reef's popular with divers, especially the treasure hunters. That wreck we saw is only one of many in these waters. That's the real reason for the name of this island." Unhooking the belt he still wore, he dropped it on the ground.

"I think I like your explanation better."

"I do, too." He grinned and the warmth in his eyes made her pulse speed up.

"I'd do anything for a cold drink." She licked her salty lips and pushed the damp hair off her forehead as she turned away from him. The more she looked at him, the more she wanted him.

Something cold nudged her arm and she looked down to see a frosted bottle of water beside her. She looked at Luke to find him watching her, a lazy smile curving his firm mouth. Right now she'd give anything to feel that mouth on hers.

Instead she picked up the bottle, surprised by a stab of resentment toward him that she couldn't keep out of her voice. "You think of everything!"

Except what she was thinking about. She quickly took a long, grateful swallow of the cold water. She needed cooling off.

He was watching her when she slowly lowered the bottle. For a moment there was something grim in the back of his eyes, but once again the impression vanished before she had time to really register it. "I try to."

Taking the bottle from her, he tipped his head back to take a long swallow of the frosty drink. She looked away, unable to bear seeing his lips where hers had been such a short while ago.

But that resolve didn't last long. Once again she stole a look. Droplets of water still clung to his golden skin and mingled with the light sprinkling of fine, dark hair on his chest. Her gaze ran over him, all lean, solid muscle in the brief black trunks, every line of his body sculpted and perfect. She pictured herself slowly pulling off his trunks, exposing him one tantalizing inch at a time...

What was she doing?

He lowered the bottle and met her gaze directly. She didn't bother looking away, shielding herself. Let him see the truth, what did it matter?

"So, what do you think of snorkeling now?"

She blinked, not prepared for the innocuousness of the question. Couldn't he see that right now she'd rather be in his arms than talking at all?

"You were right, it's very easy and a lot of fun. Thank you for inviting me."

"It was my pleasure," he said quietly.

Suddenly he tore his brooding gaze away from her and turned to stretch out on his stomach. From the pouch he pulled out the tiniest pair of binoculars she'd ever seen and lifted them to his eyes to look out to sea.

He wanted her but he was fighting it. Why? Lord knows, she wanted him, too, in a way that frightened and excited her at the same time.

Never before had she met a man who made her blood pound so savagely through her veins. Her breathing came fast and shallow, and her flesh prickled with tiny goosebumps that raised all the fine hairs on her arms. A melting heat started deep inside her that had nothing to do with the blazing Caribbean sun.

In a brazen move she stretched out close beside him.

"You were right, this really has been an adventure. Even more of an adventure than I expected."

"I'm glad you're having a good time." He didn't lower the glasses but there was no reserve now in his low, dark voice. It only left her even more confused and heightened her desire to a fevered pitch.

She sat up quickly and pulled her knees to her chest, wrapping her arms around them, trying to ignore him. But when her gaze rested on his muscular, long-limbed body stretched invitingly beside her, it was hard to resist her urge to run her hand along his muscular legs, his broad chest.

"What are you looking at?" Her voice sounded hoarse with frustration but she didn't care.

"A couple of frigate birds on the shore. Want to see?"

"Sure." She took the glasses, but her mind wasn't on the local wildlife. What she wanted was for something—*anything* to happen between them. At the same time she was miserably aware of being too much of a coward to *make* it happen.

Through the small binoculars she scanned the empty shoreline, then handed them back. "I think they flew away."

"Too bad, they're rather beautiful."

Who cared! Her nerves were stretched to screaming pitch. If he didn't touch her soon, she'd die.

Luke sat up, so abruptly that it startled her, but he only reached into his bag again. He pulled out a tube of sunblock and tossed it to her with a smile. "You'd better put some of this stuff on, or you'll fry."

She squeezed a dab of lotion onto her palm and began smoothing it over her arms. Right now, she didn't care about a sunburn. She wanted him, she wanted to feel him touching her. And suddenly she knew how to make that happen.

Artlessly, she held out the tube toward him. "Would you please put some on my back?"

A brief flash of consternation crossed his face, quickly veiled with a dispassionate smile as he took the sunblock. "Sure, turn around."

He began massaging in the cream with businesslike efficiency. He didn't linger over it, but her every sense was keenly focused on the feel of his slightly rough hands stroking her skin.

When he deftly pulled her shoulder strap aside she bit down hard on her bottom lip and closed her eyes at the melting rush of response to his touch.

"I'm glad you're enjoying yourself," he said. "You looked so tense when you arrived. I thought you needed to unwind."

Somehow he had to distract himself. He had a job to do, damn it! He couldn't let himself think about how she felt under his hands, how warm and touchable. How he'd like to slow down and take his time to explore her with his hands, his mouth.

"Yes, I suppose I did overreact a little when we met. Work has been hectic, I had to get away."

She pushed her hair up and out of the way, exposing her nape. He was so tempted to place his lips against that pale velvet skin, but he battered down the impulse. Hadn't she just told him an outright lie? But then he was lying to her, too—although that was different.

"What do you do?" he asked.

"I'm an appraiser for Summerhill's, an auction house in Toronto. We handle everything from art to furniture. My area is jewelry, mostly estate."

"A jewelry appraiser!" He realized that his fingers were gripping her shoulder, digging into the soft, smooth flesh. He forced himself to relax and continue rubbing the lotion down over her shoulder blades and the rest of her back. "How interesting. How did you ever get into that line of work?"

He knew exactly how, and he knew why, too. What an ideal pipeline for information, what a convenient profession. Oh, yes, very convenient. He compressed his lips, trying to contain the surge of anger. Why was he getting so worked up? Why was he taking her duplicity so personally?

Under his hands she shrugged carelessly, a little too carelessly. "I started out studying medieval history and working part-time at an auction house in Paris, but I became so fascinated by their estate jewelry that I ended up taking a job as assistant to the master appraiser. I learned a lot from him."

Not to mention what she learned from her father.

Something hardened inside him as he deliberately went over what he knew about Claire Sterling. Her parents divorced when she was six, her mother taking her back home to Canada while her Scottish father moved to France to carry on an extremely profitable trade on the Riviera.

Luke's mouth twisted with anger. James Sterling had never been caught. The French police had a dossier on him a foot thick, but never a shred of actual proof.

His ex-wife had died when Claire was sixteen and the girl had gone to live with her father. At that point he ostensibly gave up his life of crime and adopted a respectable front as a dealer in antique silver. Yet now it seemed Sterling was back in action, with his daughter as an accomplice. But Luke wasn't about to let them sabotage *his* operation.

"There, that should cover it." He carefully replaced the straps of her bathing suit, glad the ordeal was over.

But she turned toward him, tube in hand and a lethal smile on her soft, pink lips. "I'll do your back now."

"No!" The last thing he wanted her to do was touch him. "That won't be necessary...."

"Don't be silly, one good turn deserves another."

He tried to ignore the small flare of desire in her eyes, mixed with uncertainty. A potent aphrodisiac.

Obviously she expected some move on his part, and he had to keep up the pretense of being attracted to her. Except that it wasn't a pretense. And *that* was the dangerous part.

So he turned away from her and gritted his teeth, steeling himself against the onslaught of sensation he knew would engulf him as soon as she touched him.

After squeezing some cream onto her palm, she moved around behind him. His muscles tensed immediately at the first touch of her soft, warm hands. As she slowly massaged in the lotion he felt all his senses sharpen to an excruciating pitch.

He became aware of the shape of his back under her palms, the warmth of the sun soaking into his flesh, the way his muscles quivered beneath her gentle, mesmerizing touch, and that he was getting achingly, painfully hard. He couldn't take this anymore.

Abruptly he swung around and grabbed her wrist to stop her. She blinked up at him and with a shock he saw dreamy, bemused desire clouding her blue eyes. This was getting way out of hand.

He forced himself to smile as he let her go. "That's fine, thank you."

With a dizzy sense of relief he heard the low, droning buzz he'd been waiting for. The noise got louder and a moment later a small Cessna swung around the headland and dropped slowly toward the water, gliding in to touch down right beside the yacht.

Thank God, not a moment too soon.

He took the sunblock from Claire and threw it into the pack, then rolled away from her onto his stomach, to smother his painful erection against the hard ground.

He picked up the binoculars again. "So... have you ever been to the Caribbean before?"

"No, this is my first visit... Hey, what's that plane doing down there?"

"Dropping off a guest maybe... or supplies." He watched with satisfaction the waterproof drums being unloaded from the plane and clicked the silent shutter, making sure he got a good series of shots as they were hauled into a small launch and taken the short distance back to the yacht. That was all he needed to see.

Relief coursing through him, he quickly got to his feet and picked up the pack to cover himself. "It's getting late, we have to go now."

"I suppose we should." She was clearly disappointed.

No wonder she was confused, with all the mixed signals he'd been giving her. But for the first time in his life he was finding it incredibly difficult to keep his perspective. Was this just another symptom of the growing unease he'd been feeling lately? Was this the start of burnout? *Was* it time to quit?

She got to her feet, the white bathing suit clinging to every enticing curve and hollow of her slender body. "I wish we could stay a little longer, it's so peaceful up here."

When she said things like that, in that soft, shy way, he wanted to forget about the whole bloody lot and take her, like he wanted to so badly.

"Yeah, me, too," he lied. As far as he was concerned, they couldn't leave soon enough.

Those big blue eyes, that soft, quivering mouth, disturbed and distracted him so much. More and more all he could think about was stripping her to her bare flesh and burying himself in her right where she stood. But if he couldn't do it cold-bloodedly, he shouldn't do it at all.

Given the state he was in right now, he knew damn well he couldn't manage that. And right now he needed to be alert and focused on his purpose here. He needed to keep his wits sharp, not clouded by lust.

THE SUN HUNG LOW above Fort Charlotte as Claire stepped back onto the dock at St. Vincent, with very different feelings than when she had left only a few hours before.

After thanking Samuel and saying goodbye, they headed back along the wharf and into town. They had an hour to spend before the helicopter shuttle left for Bateaux, and decided to walk to the helipad instead of taking a taxi.

"Thank you for a lovely day, Luke. I enjoyed myself very much."

It had been wonderful, but the most frustrating day she'd spent in a long time. Luke had been charming and entertaining. And she'd bet her life that he'd been as attracted to her as she to him. So why did he suddenly switch off?

She felt thoroughly baffled as he led her through the quiet streets that he seemed to know like the back of his hand.

"I'm glad you had fun, so did I. All that hard work getting you there was worth it."

If he felt that way, then why hadn't he taken advantage of the time they'd been alone? But he hadn't, not by a single word, a single look, a single touch. He'd behaved like the perfect gentleman. Damn him.

"Will you have dinner with me tonight?"

In his eyes she saw that warmth once again, that earnestness and admiration that pushed her aching arousal up one more notch. She looked down to her sandaled feet on the dusty ground. This was unbearable, he shouldn't do this if he wasn't going to follow through.

She should say no. "I'd love to."

Suddenly he gripped her arm just above the elbow, stopping her in her tracks. Two massive men were ahead of them on the narrow street, one carrying a gun.

With a gasp, she stepped a little closer to Luke. He cocked his head, listening while he focused on the man with the gun. A soft footfall made her turn her head to see another man behind them. Fear turned her knees to jelly.

The deserted street was little more than an alley lined with closed doors of weathered boards and blind, empty windows. No one to see, no one to help.

Claire darted a frantic glance at Luke. Tension emanated from every taut line of his body, but not fear. Just a still, waiting intensity that burned in his narrowed eyes as he watched the man with the gun.

The bigger man grinned broadly and casually waved the black automatic. "You folks having a good time?"

6

HER STOMACH muscles tightened into a knot. This couldn't be what she thought it was. "We're having a lovely time, thank you. You have a very nice island here."

For a moment the man looked nonplussed, then he exchanged surprised glances with his partner and they laughed. Luke shot her a fond look of amusement tinged with exasperation.

"Thank you, we like it." The man gave a small, mocking bow. "I just hope this experience isn't going to sour your mind toward your stay here." He laughed again and the other two joined in, quietly menacingly.

"We'll be as quick as possible so you can continue your enjoyment of our beautiful sights," he said with mock solicitude, and raised his gun purposefully.

Luke let out an exasperated sigh. "Shit."

"Come on, let's have them," the man with the gun said as he waved it.

Claire glanced anxiously at Luke. He appeared calm, but his hand wrapped around her arm had tightened painfully. "We have no choice, we'd better give it to them."

The next moment he pushed her hard and she was reeling away from him. With a half turn he kicked the man behind him square in the jaw, snapping his head back to send him flying toward the nearest wall where he slumped in a heap.

At the same time he grabbed the gun by the barrel and twisted it down, his other fist smacking into the base of the gunman's throat with a sickening thud.

The third man had been watching, stunned, then roused himself to grab Luke from behind, squeezing an arm across his throat. Luke jabbed his elbow back with a force that could have cracked a few ribs. The man gasped, his eyes glazing with pain, and let go of Luke to clutch at his chest.

Quick as lightning, Luke turned, grabbed his shoulders and rammed his knee into the man's groin.

Before she knew it had begun, it was over. Dazed, Claire regarded the two men on the ground. The first man was unconscious, the other lay writhing and moaning on the broken, dirty pavement.

And Luke! Seeming completely unruffled, he casually bent down to pick up the gun. After checking it, he calmly slipped it into the waistband of his trousers. So sure and confident in his handling of a deadly weapon, when she would have been afraid to even touch the thing.

He looked over at her with a grim smile. "Are you okay?"

She nodded, still a little dazed.

"Good, then let's get out of here." Grabbing her arm, he pulled her quickly down the alley.

As she hurried along beside him, she looked back over her shoulder at the three huddled forms. "What about those men? Are we just going to leave them there?"

"I don't think they're ready to get up yet."

She stared at Luke in amazement. His hair a little tousled, his white shirt only slightly askew, he looked no more the worse for wear than any tourist after a day of sight-seeing. As if he hadn't single-handedly incapacitated three massive, dangerous men. And with such deadly efficiency she barely saw it happen, even though her horror-filled gaze hadn't left him for a moment.

"Shouldn't we at least report the incident to the police?"

"And miss our ride back? Don't be silly." He shot her a cool smile, never slackening his determined stride.

She smiled weakly back, her mind reeling. Who was this man? He was as cool about that dangerous encounter as if it were an everyday occurrence. Cool, but deadly purposeful. His movements had been so quick, so focused, so economical—so lethal. She felt a small shiver of fear.

As they came to the end of the alley he pulled out the gun and tossed it carelessly into a huge garbage can standing outside the back door of a restaurant.

His mouth twitched in a grim smile. "Good place for it, don't you think?"

"Think! I don't know what to think anymore."

"Poor darling, it's been a little rough on you, hasn't it?"

"That's an understatement," she said softly.

"Never mind, a hot shower and a good meal will put you to rights again." This time his smile was warm and understanding.

"Don't bet on it." The past seventy-two hours had been filled with one nightmarish incident after another.

"Bet on it? I guarantee it!" He slipped his hard arm around her shoulders and gave her a reassuring squeeze, then kept it there as they walked along.

A small shudder of desire went through her at his touch. In her confused mind one thing stood out clearly. In his own way, Luke was as brutal and ruthless an animal as those thugs. His bad side wasn't a place *she* ever wanted to be. She'd sensed that dangerous quality in him from the very beginning, but now her instincts had been all too shockingly affirmed.

So why didn't that scare her? Even worse, why did it thrill her? Was that perverse? Why, instead of running like hell, did she want to snuggle into his arms and lose herself in his kiss?

On the trip back they shared the helicopter with another couple. Sitting silently beside him, close but not touching, she still felt dazed, while Luke made small talk with the others as if nothing had happened.

Five seconds after getting off the helicopter she couldn't even remember what the other couple looked like, but her stupor didn't prevent her from being acutely conscious of Luke. His proximity made her vibrate with burning need, crave the satisfaction she knew he, and only he, could give her. These unbridled desires were driving her crazy. She was in the middle of something she didn't understand.

Back at the hotel Luke walked her to her room. They stopped in front of her door and he looked down at her, a small, intimate smile warming his eyes.

Only a foot away, he seemed so commanding, in a way that almost intimidated her and yet compelled her to want to move closer. He roused all her senses to an exquisite pitch. As she breathed in the scent of him—the smell of the outdoors, of sea, sun and fresh air. As aggressively vital and elemental as the man himself.

"It's seven o'clock. I'll pick you up at eight-thirty for dinner. Will that be all right?"

No, that would not be all right. She didn't want to wait until eight-thirty. She wanted him to come in right now and forget about dinner. What she was hungry for couldn't be found in the dining room.

But all she said was, "That'll be fine."

Right there and then, she decided that she wouldn't let this evening end without having him.

Could this really be her? This predatory, aggressive woman? She'd never felt like this before. This was a phase she didn't recognize at all. She'd turned a corner into foreign territory.

She gazed up into his eyes and found them dark and intense, filled with a steely determination that gave her a tremor of doubt. But the next moment his mouth curved in a smile and his expression lightened.

He picked up her hand and kissed her fingers. The tingling went right up her arm, straight to her heart, making it beat erratically against her ribs.

"Thanks for a lovely day," he said softly. "I'll see you in a little while." Then he turned and walked to his room.

Claire shivered with excited anticipation as she also let herself in and shut the door. She jumped when she saw a man sitting in the chair by the window, his long legs outstretched, hands clasped loosely across his waist.

Startled, she clutched a hand to her chest. "You scared the living daylights out of me. How did you get in here?"

James stood, chuckling, and came toward her. "I'm not as rusty as you think I am."

He planted a kiss on her forehead and she smelled the clean familiar scent of English Leather soap. He was wearing black tie and looking so handsome that she felt pride and exasperation all at the same time.

"I still have a few tricks up my sleeve." His smile was smug as he turned and sauntered back to drape himself on the couch.

She aimed a penetrating look at him. "I'm sure you do, but I don't want to know what they are."

She walked from the sitting area into the alcove where the bed stood. "I'll only worry, and after what I've already been through I don't need you to tell me not to be a fool, in that annoying way you have."

"Fair enough."

His meek agreement didn't fool her. She looked over at him to see the mocking amusement in his eyes and she gritted her teeth.

"Are you going out tonight?" he asked.

"I have a date for dinner."

"With Luke Dalton?" Sitting on the couch, he was absently playing with the whiskers of his beard and watching her through narrowed eyes.

"Yes. With Luke Dalton." She tensed, ready to leap to Luke's defense, and the realization took her aback. "Is there something wrong with that?"

"Maybe, maybe not," he murmured, and gave her an assessing look through narrowed lids.

She knew that look well, and she hated it. It always foreshadowed something she wasn't going to like or agree with. Like the time he'd bet his antique business on the turn of a card because he needed capital and couldn't raise any more money.

"You spent the day with this man. What have you learned about him?" he asked bluntly.

"He's the most enigmatic, exciting man I've ever met." *And I want him so badly I can hardly stand it.* A faint heat climbed her cheeks and she bowed her head to hide it from her father's shrewd gaze. "He's...he's also very nice."

A snort of disgust brought him to his feet and toward her. "Nice! Come on, Claire, you know what I mean. Where's he from, what does he do? Or say he does," he finished cynically.

"Isn't it a little late to be playing the interfering, overly protective father?" she said with a laugh.

He stopped in front of her and there was no laughter in his eyes now. "I have a good reason for asking. What do you know about him?" His tone was deadly serious.

Claire felt a small flutter of anxiety. "Well, he's English...he comes from a small town in Yorkshire, but he lives and works in London." She began ticking off the points on her fingers. "His father is dead, mother is still alive. He has two brothers and two sisters."

She racked her brains for anything else Luke had mentioned, then snapped her fingers. "Oh...and he's a banker."

James burst out in contemptuous laughter and she pressed her lips together angrily.

"What's so funny?" she said through clenched teeth.

"A banker!"

He shook his head and chuckled into his hand, obviously amused at her naïveté.

"If he's a banker, I'm Donald Trump!"

James started chuckling again. "How any child of mine could be so gullible is beyond me."

"If you came here to annoy me, you've done it. Now go away and let me get ready for my date."

"I came here to warn you." He turned back to her and there was no humor left in his face at all. It looked hard and frightening, like the face of a stranger, and Claire felt tension prickle the back of her neck. "Be careful of Luke Dalton. He's not what he appears to be."

"What do you mean?"

For a long moment he just looked at her without saying anything.

Finally he said, "I think he may be the fly in the ointment, our competition."

"You...you think...Luke Dalton is the jewel thief?" She stared at him for a moment as if she'd never seen him before. "No! No, that's impossible!"

In reply, he raised a cool eyebrow at her impassioned defense. His gaze swept over her flushed face, then his eyes narrowed. "What's the matter? You look a little odd."

"I'm fine." But she wasn't fine, her heart was pounding so hard it hurt. The very idea was preposterous, but in a frightening way it made sense. It answered so many puzzling questions. "How do you know this?"

He shrugged, an elegant gesture of his black-clad shoulders in the impeccably tailored dinner jacket. "Sixth sense. It's easy to recognize other professionals."

"So you don't have any actual proof?" She jumped at the thinnest of straws.

"No. I don't have any actual proof."

But I might. Her mind went back unwillingly to the previous night when Luke had caught her on his balcony. He'd been dressed in black casual wear, but earlier that evening he'd been wearing a tux. The thief had been dressed all in black, too.

"I want you to keep an eye on him." James's hard voice brought her back from the ridiculous path her thoughts were taking. "If he is our man, we're going to have to make sure he doesn't get to that coronet before we do."

"That's a big *if*. You have no earthly reason to suspect Luke Dalton." And neither did she, she reminded herself sternly. "You could be, and probably are, barking up the wrong tree."

"Maybe, but all the same, I'd like you to watch him."

She felt a shiver of distaste. "Watch him? What... what do you mean? Spy on him?"

"I mean, watch him," James amplified impatiently. "Occupy him. He's attracted to you already, that can only be to our advantage. If he is our man it'll give him less time to devote to his work and buy *me* more time to locate the coronet."

"I don't know if I can do that," she said slowly. It was one thing spending time with him because she wanted to. What James was asking her to do was tantamount to lying.

But could it be true? Could Luke be the—no! Her mind revolted at the idea, but on the other hand...

It made more sense that Luke could be a thief than a banker. She'd seen ample evidence that he had nerves of steel, strength, determination and single-minded intensity. Right from the beginning she'd sensed that this man spelled danger. Had her instincts been trying to tell her that he was a criminal all along? Perhaps she'd inherited more from her father than she'd ever realized until this moment.

But it couldn't be true about Luke. Why not? Because he'd made her aware of the depth of her own sexuality for the first time in her life? Because he made her yearn to explore it? She wanted to taste that heady excitement, experience it, but if he was just a common thief...

"You have to try, Claire." James was quietly, deadly serious. "This man could jeopardize everything if he is who I think he is. You already have an in with him..." He stopped suddenly, grim and alert. "He didn't *do* anything to you, anything that hurt you, did he? Is that why you don't want to do this?"

She shook her head. "Please—I just met the man."

He raised an incredulous eyebrow. "I didn't think you were so naive."

She lifted her chin defensively. "I'm not. The point is, I'm no Mata Hari. I don't know the first thing about being a spy."

James heaved an impatient sigh. "Look, you're the one who wanted to help me. Are you going to do it or not?"

"Yes," she insisted. "I want to help you, but I just don't think he could be the man. *My* instincts tell me that—"

"Your instincts!" he said derisively. "Let's face it, my dear, you're a collector of stray dogs. What about that Pete character?"

"You mean Paul," she corrected. Her father took perverse delight in never getting his name right.

"Paul, Pete, what's the difference! Where were your instincts then? The man was a gormless twit, and it was your own damn fault you got hurt."

"Thanks for your support and understanding." Her sarcasm had no effect; he just gave her a bland look. "Anyway, Paul's got nothing to do with it. That was over months ago."

The breakup had been really hard because Paul had claimed she'd deceived him by leading him to believe she was the kind of person who wanted the same things he wanted—money, influence, mixing in the glittering social circles that could advance his law career.

But he was the one who'd betrayed her. It had begun with separate vacations and ended the day he'd left her. He'd got married less than a month later to one of *her* wealthy clients.

"Well, thank God for that," James said impatiently. "I was getting sick of hearing about Paul. I told you from the beginning he wasn't good enough for you."

She gave him a wry smile. "You don't think anybody's good enough for me."

James's mouth quirked under the mustache. "True. The trouble is, you always pick the losers."

"No, they weren't losers. But they were weak," she found herself admitting for the first time. "I thought they needed me. Everybody needs to be needed."

It hit her like a sledgehammer. Why had she never seen it before? Even though, by the time she came to live with him, James had given up his illegal pursuits, he still had all the qualities that had enabled him to carry out his crimes—strength, determination, ruthlessness. Consciously or not, had she been deliberately avoiding men like her father?

Until Luke Dalton. But that was different.

"I've learned my lesson," she said. "I'm going to go for what I want. What I need."

The trouble was that what she wanted, what she needed right now, was Luke. If he was a thief, how could she continue to feel this way? How could she contemplate using his body? But all she wanted to do was satisfy this craving and then for once walk away, free of the heartache and the emotional baggage she was usually left with. And this time she could probably do it and get away with it.

"Now that's more like a daughter of mine, instead of all that whining you've subjected me to these past months."

She ignored the gibe. Paul had never inspired that bone-melting awareness that just one small smile from Luke could cause. And Luke hadn't even kissed her yet! God knows what that would do to her. She bit her lower lip and suppressed a shiver.

"But we're getting away from the point," James continued relentlessly. "Are you going to keep an eye on Luke Dalton?"

She wanted to say no, that Luke was innocent. But a small voice taunted that her father's annoying hunches all too often proved to be true. After all, right from the beginning she'd sensed something dangerous and hard about Luke.

All at once she felt intensely depressed. When it came to men, she was obviously a terrible judge of character.

"Of course I'm going to do it," she told her father reluctantly. But not tonight. She just couldn't face him tonight.

LUKE KNOCKED at the white louvered door again and listened, a frown creasing his brow. He knew James had been with her, and obviously this no-show had something to do with that. Did he have her out on a job?

His jaw tightened with anger. Despite himself he felt a nagging concern. What if she got caught? What if she got hurt? Damn it, why should he care? That would only make his job easier.

What if she got herself killed?

The thought filled him with cold dread and he spun away from the door with a sharp expulsion of breath.

No, he wouldn't cloud the issue with any of that nonsense.

He began to retrace his steps. This was the perfect opportunity to search her room. He clamped down on his jaw so hard it hurt, but he welcomed the pain. It was better than guilt.

He had to remember she was a liar and a thief. It didn't matter that every time he looked at her he wanted to make love to her. If having sex with her could get him what he wanted, then he'd do it. He could no longer allow himself to be distracted from doing what he had to do.

Grimly, purposefully, he let himself back into his room, walked straight through and out onto the balcony. He stopped short and the breath caught in his throat.

Two rooms away, Claire was standing out on her own terrace. Against the dark, tropic night, she glowed pale in the moonlight, a slim, ethereal figure, her brief, white shirt gently molded to her curves by the breeze, her pale blond hair tumbled around her shoulders. So enticing, so maddening.

Clutching the railing, she leaned toward the distant ocean, with something so yearning and vulnerable about her that he had to coldly and deliberately harden himself against it.

Any response to her would be fatal. Quickly he climbed over the rail and leapt across to the other balcony.

STARING OUT at the ocean, at the path of shining pewter moonlight beyond the black silhouettes of the palms, Claire felt weighed down with gloom. Conflicting thoughts battered each other until her mind was numb. She just wanted to wake up and find this was all a dream, after all.

Luke couldn't be a jewel thief, he was just too wonderful. But then, why did the idea make so much sense? Besides, if that were true, then how could her father have been a thief? He was a wonderful man, too—kind, caring, everything she admired in a man, and hadn't found yet.

No, the evidence against Luke, thin as it was, was just too convincing. By his own admission, he'd stolen her passport, so slickly that she never even noticed. Last night he could have been the figure entering Maisie's room. He could easily have stolen her jewels, slipped out by her front door, down the hall into his own room and walked out onto his balcony a few moments later. And then the way he'd dealt with those thugs...

But it was all circumstantial, she reminded herself fiercely. And yet it could also add up to him being exactly what James suspected. If that were true, then how could she feel this way about a thief? Yet if she believed him innocent, why was she filled with doubt and suspicion?

She sighed in frustration and gripped the railing tighter. *Steady on*. Here she was convicting him on nothing more than her father's hunch, when there was every possibility James was wrong. But her small spurt of optimism fluttered and died. If she believed that, then why was she already acting as if he was guilty?

A tiny scraping noise made her turn her head to see Luke standing on the next balcony. Her heart leapt and began to pound with a mixture of fear and excitement as she watched him vault over the rail and jump effortlessly across the gap to land on the outer ledge of her balcony.

Instead of climbing over, he stayed on the outside of the railing, one arm casually wrapped around the support pole, apparently uncaring that he was four stories above the ground.

In the soft light from her room she watched his eyes, lazy and gleaming, drinking their fill of her from her toes on up to her face, lingering for a heart-stopping moment on her mouth.

"You didn't answer my knock and I was worried about you." His low voice was as dark and soft as the tropic night.

'So you just decided to hop a few balconies and come and find out if I was all right." Trying for dry sarcasm, all she managed was a husky croak.

What did it say for her morals if she could still be attracted to a man who could be a thief?

A slow smile curved his hard lips. "Well, I did get the idea from you, after all." His smile widened, exposing his even, white teeth and sending eddies of pleasure rippling along her flesh. "And you're definitely worth taking the risk for."

Now he wasn't teasing anymore. An aura of compelling seductiveness surrounded her, reached out and pulled her in.

What did morals have to do with it? She'd never been so consumed by her physical hunger, and she didn't want to fight it anymore. But damn it, she *had* to.

"Wouldn't you be ticked off if you fell and broke your neck, all for a woman you hardly know?" She tried to sound dry and cynical, struggling in vain to knock out the ancient magic and bring this thing down to earth. It was all as fantastic as *A Midsummer Night's Dream*, complete with the fool—her.

"I know more about you than you think."

His words gave her a guilty start, until she realized this was just flirtatious chitchat. *Yeah, well I may know more about you than you think.* But she'd give anything for James to be wrong. Then she could just surrender to this fantasy.

"Like what?" She shivered with trepidation, but turned more fully toward him.

For a moment he just stood on the other side of the railing, looking at her, his eyes gleaming in the light from her room.

"Like, for instance, that you're sweet and caring, and it shows in your baby blue eyes." Slowly he climbed over the wrought-iron railing and moved toward her. She held her breath. "But you're strong-willed and sometimes a little stubborn, I think. I can see that in your mouth, that willfulness, and yet it doesn't make your lips one bit less kissable." He stopped, inches away. She could feel the heat of his body, so close, see the hunger in his eyes.

Without meaning to, she licked her dry lips. Something flared in his eyes and a slow burning spread through her. What she'd been yearning for was within her grasp and it was too damn late. She wouldn't let herself forget the possibility of him being a thief. But at the same time she wanted to pay him back a little for the frustration he'd put her through all afternoon. See him squirm while she tantalized him.

"And what about my ears? You didn't say anything about my ears yet."

"Your ears..." With one fingertip he traced the curve of her ear, and just that small contact was exquisite torture. Then he bent to brush his lips over the path his fingertip had taken and took the lobe between his teeth, gently biting down. Every nerve ending exploded with sensation, wildly out of proportion to the cause. "Your ears... drive me wild."

With one shaking hand she gently pushed him away. Damn him, when he didn't want anything to happen, nothing happened. But when she tried to turn the tables, he was still the one calling the shots.

"I find this very confusing." She tried to sidestep him, but his hands were now cupping her shoulders and sliding slowly, distractingly, devastatingly down her arms. The palms were rough and callused but his touch inflamed her, a delicious abrasion on her sensitized skin. "I got the impression this afternoon that you weren't interested."

He brought her swaying toward him as his lips grazed across her cheek. "This afternoon you were virtually at my mercy, in a very vulnerable position. It wouldn't have been very gentlemanly of me." His hot breath fanned her face and she closed her eyes.

"And tonight?" she breathed as his mouth hovered excruciatingly at the corner of her lips.

"Tonight... you can escape, if you want to. Do you want to escape, Claire?" His voice slid over her, soft and deep and throbbing with desire.

"Yes..." But she couldn't help herself as she turned her head and at long last felt his warm lips close on hers.

7

As their lips met his arms went around her completely, pulling her close against him with ferocity. Her arms slid up around his neck as she strained against him, her nipples hard and painful as she pressed against his chest, against the smooth fabric of the tuxedo.

His hands slowly dropped to her hips, sending a deep, slow shiver racing through her body as she felt his fingers inching up the hem of her nightshirt, his hands cupping her bottom and squeezing, bringing her up against him. He groaned into her mouth and the erotic sound sent her heightened senses skyrocketing.

What had happened to her determination to ignore her libido? This man could be a thief. But then, the evidence condemning him was flimsy and circumstantial. She ignored the nagging little voice that said that was only an excuse for giving in to lust. Besides, by giving in, perhaps she could exorcise this consuming hunger and get on with her life.

She laced one hand through his hair at the back of his head while she slipped the other inside his jacket and around to caress his back, to feel the muscles moving under the crisp shirt. As his hips pressed against her, she could feel his erection.

Suddenly he stiffened and pushed her away.

Confused, dazed, she stared at him across the few feet separating them. "Luke... what's the matter?"

He was breathing fast and in the light from the room she could see his face was flushed, his eyes glittering, but his expression was masked. Then a small, derisive smile curved one corner of his mouth. "I think we should go have dinner."

She could see the enormous effort it took to keep his voice even, and knew he was as affected as she. The knowledge frustrated and emboldened her.

"I don't want to have dinner," she murmured, and moved toward him.

She reached out, but he caught her wrist before she could touch him and held it in a firm grip. She could feel the slight tremor in his body as he looked down at her with those compelling eyes of his.

"But I do," he said firmly. "Now, be a good girl and go and get dressed."

He gave her a little push to send her on her way, but instead she turned back to him, determined to get some answers.

"Why?"

He raised an eyebrow in mock surprise. "Why? Because people might laugh if you went to dinner in your nightshirt."

"That's not what I mean. You more or less invited that kiss. You want me right now, I can see it..." She walked closer and put a hand on his chest. His muscles tensed under her palm and a small, smug smile curved her lips. "I can feel it in the way your body trembles. So why?"

He grabbed her wrist again, stopping her hand from sliding up the broad expanse of his chest.

"I'll tell you why," he said laconically. "Because I'm the type of man who likes to decide on the time and place... and woman. And right now I want to go to dinner."

"Are you trying to tell me you're not interested?" What was his game now?

A small sigh escaped him. "No, I'm trying to tell you that I'm starved." He smiled and there was a hint of derision to his hard mouth. "Now, please, go get dressed."

"If you insist." Still confused, she bit her lip. "But I'm warning you, the evening isn't over yet."

Now his smile broadened with real amusement. "Is that a challenge, Claire?"

"No, it's a warning." Determined now, she smiled back, her intention perfectly serious. "I have to take a quick shower."

"Then do it. I'll wait here." He let go of her wrist and folded his arms across his chest, leaning back against the balcony railing.

"Are you always so bossy?"

"Always. And you?"

"Ye—very funny!" She gave him a wry grimace then turned and walked back through the sliding-glass doors into her room.

Letting out a massive sigh of relief, Luke turned to look out over the darkened grounds below, shaken.

This wasn't the first time he'd romanced a woman in the "line of duty," but this was the first time he'd lost control like that. Forgotten why he was here, forgotten who he was, in the need to just take her, right there.

A hand automatically went to his breast pocket and found it empty. His mouth twisted in a wry smile. Two months since he quit, but old habits died hard, particularly at times like this. And he'd been so proud of kicking it so easily.

Claire Sterling could drive a man to forget everything. She was driving this particular man crazy. There, he'd admitted it.

If she'd turned out to be the hardened bitch he'd first pegged her as, things would have been simple. How could she also be the warm and sensitive person he'd discovered?

To his surprise he'd found himself enjoying her wry sense of humor, and admiring her guts in tackling something that obviously made her nervous. He hadn't been prepared for her ingenuous admission that she trusted him. And even more surprising, he believed her. He, who knew better than anybody, that there was no honor among thieves.

But then, maybe he was wrong about her. Maybe she knew nothing about her father's business here. Maybe the earth was flat. My God, was that what she reduced him to, clutching at straws? Maybe he really was losing his edge.

With a cold, creeping fear, he knew he wouldn't be able to resist her for long. He just hoped to God he could keep things in perspective, not do anything to jeopardize his purpose here.

INSTEAD OF GOING to the dining room, Luke told her they were going to the beachside pavilion restaurant.

As they walked out into the warm night air she allowed her glance to slide over to the man beside her, so tall, so distinctively handsome in his tux. He moved with a lithe grace, incredible for such a big man.

At five-eight she was fairly tall, but next to him she felt petite. It wasn't a feeling she was accustomed to, but she could get used to it. The thought made her lips curve in a smile.

As she walked through the grounds by Luke's side, down a path softly lit with lanterns, Claire felt as if she were walking through a dream. In spite of the other people they passed, she felt as if she were cocooned in a place where only she and Luke existed. The velvety warm darkness was filled with the heady, tangled fragrance of the tropics—hibiscus, frangipani, and a hundred other blooms perfuming the night, only for them.

The soft music of a steel band floated toward them on the same breeze that fluttered over her white slip dress, brushing the brief sliver of silk caressingly over her bare legs with intoxicatingly delicate sensuality.

Her diamond pendant felt cool against her breastbone and her long hair brushed over the thin straps of her dress to sweep her shoulders, sending small shivers racing over her bare skin.

She smiled, a slow, secret smile. Every inch of her body tingled with heightened awareness, delicious anticipation.

"A penny for your thoughts."

The sound of his low voice made her turn her head to find Luke watching her, a lazy smile on his lips. But something in his face gave her the impression of tension.

She was tired of all the hidden messages and meanings. For once she wanted to be honest, where it was possible to be honest. "I was thinking about how good we'd be together when we finally get around to making love."

He gave a sharp gasp, but when he spoke he sounded lazily amused and a little mocking. "There you go presuming again."

At that she only smiled. The sudden flare of desire in his eyes had given him away. *He* was thinking about it, too.

Through a grove of palms ahead she could see the mellow lights illuminating an open pavilion right down by the shore. An intimate, impossibly romantic setting.

As they got closer she saw that the pavilion held only a dozen or so tables. Walking up the steps, she noticed James immediately, at a table for two with Nikki Jones, of all people.

Nikki was leaning on one elbow, listening to James with rapt fascination. Claire felt a surge of impatience with her father. For God's sake, couldn't he at least stick to women his own age!

But a moment later she realized why she felt so annoyed. Seeing James had reminded her of her assignment. She was irked with her father for putting her in this uncomfortable position of lying to Luke.

Yet, if Luke *was* what her father suspected, it would be all right to lie to him, wouldn't it? But what if he was innocent?

Clashing thoughts went chasing around her head until she thought she'd scream from frustration. She was going to drive herself crazy if she kept on like this.

All she could do was continue keeping Luke busy, as her father had asked, but she wasn't going to spend another second agonizing over the possibility of him being a thief. Even if it had been motivated by rampant lust, she'd decided he was innocent until proven otherwise and she'd stick with her decision.

This was the new Claire Sterling. It might be twenty years too late, but damn it, she was finally joining the sexual revolution! She was giving herself permission to enjoy this time with Luke. She'd deal with anything else as and when it came up.

On that thought she walked right past James's table without even a glance in his direction.

During dinner Claire set out to learn as much as she could about the man at her side. Not because her father wanted her to, but because Luke intrigued and fascinated her. And because she was bound and determined to know more about the man she was going to end up in bed with before the night was through.

Once again Luke was the perfect companion, answering her questions about himself with relaxed good humor. But just as he had done that afternoon, he somehow managed to always turn the conversation back to her—her home, her friends, her job.

So she told him how she loved her downtown condo overlooking Front Street; that her best friend had married and moved to Vancouver, and that since the breakup with Paul she'd lost interest in going out very much. And as for her job—it made up for her current lack of social life.

Luke leaned on one elbow and stirred sugar into his coffee. "Paul... ex-boyfriend... husband?"

"Boyfriend... thank God I wasn't stupid enough to marry him... not that he asked me." She couldn't help the tinge of bitterness that crept into her voice. But now she knew it was only wounded ego.

"So, are you still nursing a broken heart?" His voice was casual and he kept his gaze trained on his right hand as he toyed with the coffee spoon. But once again she sensed the tension in him and something warm began to unfurl inside her.

"No, not at all," she said quietly, fiddling with her own teaspoon. "Since I've been here I haven't even thought about him, and I'm sure I don't have to tell you why."

His head jerked up and she met his suddenly enlightened gaze. A knowing look, as if he'd glimpsed into her soul. It made her feel a little shy and vulnerable, but she *wanted* him to know her. It must be remnants of the provincial values of her upbringing that made her feel it was wrong to share something so intimate with a complete stranger.

"Well, that explains a lot." His tone was dismissive.

"Hold on a minute, don't be so quick to jump to the obvious conclusion." Her shyness evaporated, replaced by impatience. "You're wrong. I'm not on the rebound and I didn't come here looking for romance."

"What did you come looking for?" he shot back quickly, taking her by surprise.

Damn her big mouth. "I told you before, just some rest and relaxation." He gave a skeptical look and she continued. "And as for this attraction I obviously feel for you . . . I just want you to know that I've never done anything like this before. But I suppose you can tell. I'm rather inept." She looked down at the tablecloth.

"On the contrary, you're doing just fine."

She heard the suppressed laughter in his voice and looked up to see bright amusement in his eyes.

"So tell me, if you don't make a habit of this sort of thing, why now? Why me?"

She shrugged and shook her head. "I don't know. I've been asking myself the same question. I mean, you're not my type."

"And what is your type?"

"Well, Paul was blond, for a start, and not quite as . . . aggressive as you are."

He raised one eyebrow and gave her a droll look.

"Maybe it's because there's something so mysterious about you."

He laughed. "There's nothing mysterious about me."

"You never talk about yourself. Whenever I try to find out about you, you change the subject."

He laughed again. "Well, there's no mystery about that. There's not much to tell. I'm afraid a banker's life is not very exciting. It's not very nice to bore young women on holiday with talk of rising interest rates, what's happening at the Federal Reserve this week and the state of the Nikkei Index. See, your eyes are glazing over already."

She tipped her head to one side and gave him a skeptical look. "Come on, everyone has more to their lives than just their jobs. Like vacations, hobbies, friends..."

"Let me see, I have no hobbies because I spend all my time working, much to my poor, gray-haired mother's chagrin. Fortunately she has four other children who aren't such a disappointment to her. Holidays—very few and far between. And when I'm on holiday, like now, I don't like to talk about my uneventful life back home."

She laughed. "Okay, you've convinced me, you're a very boring person."

But then she sobered. He still really hadn't told her about himself. Was he hiding from something? Was he trying to forget someone? She might never find out, but did it matter anyway?

"Boring or not, I've never met anybody like you before. And I may never meet anybody like you again. I may never feel like this again. For once I'm going to go for the experience and find out what it would be like to be made love to by a man like you." She took a deep breath, glad she'd got that off her chest.

For a long moment he didn't speak or look at her, but he had a curious smile on his face. Then he looked up and his smile became tinged with bitterness. "A man like me," he murmured almost to himself, with a laugh that held no humor.

Then his smile softened, making his eyes glow in the candlelight. "What can I say, Claire?" *Say you feel the same way I do.* "I'm flattered... and humbled."

A small sigh escaped her. Well, at least flattered, not to mention humbled, was better than amused. Or worse, bored.

No, the warmth that filled his eyes told her clearly that it was neither. But in spite of his obvious interest, he *still* hadn't made the slightest move to touch her.

After the meal Luke suggested they go to the casino. Like the night before, it was crowded under the bright lights, the air filled with the noise of slot machines, the acrid smell of cigarette smoke and heavy, expensive perfume.

In spite of having lived on the French Riviera for three years, she'd never visited any of the famous casinos. Partly because for most of that time she had been a minor, but also because they were James's former hunting grounds. She couldn't bring herself to visit the scenes of the crimes.

They passed into the more subdued rooms where croupiers presided over green baize tables. Not knowing how to play, she decided to watch as Luke sat down at the chemin de fer, stacked his red chips in front him and tossed one onto the table.

Her gaze darted around the faces at the table. On the other side sat a heavy, older man, his balding forehead creased with worry, as if his whole fortune were at stake. Which might not be far from the truth. Next to him, a thin, middle-aged woman in a beaded black gown bit her lip and hesitated before throwing in her own chips.

And then she looked at Luke's inscrutable, relaxed face, watching the croupier deal the cards. As the game went on she watched his stack of chips rapidly multiply, but Luke still maintained that lazy, uncaring attitude, repeatedly betting everything, except the hundred dollar chip he'd started out with.

Finally, when he had several large stacks of chips in front of him, he stood. "That's enough for me. Thank you very much." He inclined his head in a gesture that included the whole table.

Picking up a chip, he flipped it casually toward the dealer who snagged it expertly in midair, a big smile breaking out on his dark face.

"Thank you, sir." The man tucked the chip into the pocket of his red waistcoat and handed Luke a black velvet bag.

Claire's eyes widened as Luke shoveled his winnings into the bag. "You must have ten thousand dollars there!"

He shrugged and smiled. "Roughly, give or take a thousand." His blue wolf eyes gleamed with amusement at her amazement. He held one of the stacks toward her. "For you."

"What!" She took a startled step back and gave a small, embarrassed laugh. "Don't be silly, I can't take all this money!"

"Why not?" he asked casually. "You brought me luck."

"Then buy me a drink."

"No, take it." He shrugged again. "Easy come, easy go. Consider it found money."

"Nobody finds this much money. Or gives it away."

He must make a lot of money in banking. Or... If he were what her father suspected he would have this casual attitude to money, wouldn't he? After all, he didn't have to work for it.

Claire pulled herself up short. Hadn't she already decided he was innocent until proven guilty?

"Whether I win or lose or give it away, I'm not out of pocket. I still have my original investment."

But he was so breathtakingly cavalier, she could hardly believe it.

He took her hand, placed the stack of chips in her palm and closed his own hand around it. "Please accept this, Claire." His voice was deep and quiet with sincerity.

"But, Luke..." she said doubtfully.

"I insist." And that settled the matter.

Taking the winnings over to the cashier, they cashed in the chips for a stack of American dollars. Claire turned away from the booth, laughing incredulously at the pile of bills in her hand, and almost walked straight into a woman in a flame red chiffon gown.

Startled, she looked up to see a familiar face and her smile got even bigger. "Maisie! How nice to see you."

The older woman patted her arm. "Claire, dear, I'm so glad to see you. I wanted to thank you for your help this morning."

She shrugged. "I didn't do anything."

"No, you were a great comfort, wasn't she, Morris, dear?" She turned to speak loudly into her husband's ear and the old man nodded vaguely and smiled at Claire. "Don't mind Morris, he's still a little dazed. We won some money at the roulette table." She held out a small stack of blue chips and laughed. "We never win anything, do we, dear?" she trilled into Morris's ear.

Claire had to smile at her ingenuous enjoyment of life. In spite of the morning's upset, Maisie was still so sweet and gracious. But Claire couldn't help noticing the string of faux pearls around her neck, the strain behind her smile and the sadness in her eyes.

Maisie looked past her and held out her hand. "Hello, I don't believe we've met. I'm Maisie Fleming, this is my husband Morris."

"Luke Dalton."

As she watched Luke smiling and shaking hands with Maisie the realization hit her like a bucket of cold water. *He* could be that man. And if he was, how could he be so callous?

She let out an exasperated sigh. She was doing it again.

"Have you heard any more about your lovely jewels, Mrs. Fleming?" He sounded so sincere, so kindly.

"The management said they're doing everything possible to reclaim them." Her smile became wobbly and her eyes misted over. "They were Morris's present to me on the day we were married."

Something hard and ruthless appeared on Luke's face. "I'm sure they'll be recovered. This is a very small island."

He turned to look at her and Claire met his eyes to find them glittering with deep-seated anger. Why? Once again she found him so utterly baffling.

"You're very kind." Maisie flashed him a brave smile. "And now we'd better cash these in and I'll take Morris upstairs. It's way past his bedtime."

After bidding them good-night, they headed out of the casino, Claire still puzzling over the harsh look on

Luke's face. Was he angry with her for some reason? But she hadn't done anything. She let out a deep, frustrated breath. The man was such an enigma.

Passing through the carved Thai columns of the lobby, Luke took her into The Grotto, a dimly lit bar with rough stone walls and a smooth jazz quartet.

As they sat listening to music and sipping drinks at a small round table tucked into a corner, Luke nodded toward the bar. "Hey, isn't that your poolside admirer from last night?"

She looked over to see Howie, draped all over a tall, well-dressed redhead sitting on the bar stool beside him, and couldn't help but smile. "Why don't you go and rescue her? She looks as annoyed as I felt last night."

"I'm not in the business of rescuing damsels in distress, not really."

Claire tipped her head and smiled coquettishly. "Oh, was I a special case?"

"You could say so." The warmth flared in his eyes again, but he turned his gaze back to the bar. "Anyway, the lady looks like she doesn't need any help."

She looked over in time to see the redhead give her unwanted admirer a push that sent him sprawling off the bar stool. "Poor Howie. Seems he isn't having any more luck tonight."

"Poor Howie!" He shook his head in amused exasperation.

"Well, he's a pest, but I think basically harmless."

"If you say so." Luke shrugged.

But it wasn't Howie and his problems picking up women that concerned her right now; it was Luke. All evening he'd been the perfect date, but his restraint toward her was palpable. He hadn't touched her once. And yet she knew he wanted her, she could tell by the way he looked at her, by his very restraint itself, as if he dared not touch her for fear of losing control.

How she knew all this was a mystery. His face was an inscrutable mask, giving nothing away. And yet something about him, some tension that clung to him, communicated itself to her.

Of course there was no denying what she felt, what she wanted. She didn't even try. And she was determined to get what she wanted before the evening ended. This sudden aggression shocked her—where had it come from?

Finally the band finished their last set and the waiters were beginning to close up the bar. It was time to return to her room. As they rose from the small table she could sense Luke's tension increasing beneath the urbane exterior, and it gave her an unaccustomed sense of power.

He wanted her, she wanted him, but he was fighting against it. Who was going to win?

In silence he walked her back to her room, close beside her but not touching. She felt the tension he radiated mounting with each step as they got closer, enclosing them in a silent place, loud with all the unspoken emotions, the air quivering with awareness sparking between them like an electrical charge.

Stopping outside her door, she took the key from her purse. Luke stood beside her, she could feel his silent resistance.

Slowly she turned to him and lifted her gaze to his face. It was a rigid mask, his eyes carefully wiped clean of any expression, a small smile curving his lips.

Any moment now he was going to walk away and leave her. But she had other plans. Half-shocked, half-amused to find she could be so predatory, Claire discovered she was also unembarrassed.

He wanted her, she knew it. And she'd never wanted anyone like this. Never felt this blazing excitement at the very thought of touching him, of having him touch her. If she didn't do this, she'd always regret not finding out what it could be like.

Holding his gaze, she saw something almost like fear flicker in the back of his eyes. She dismissed the thought. She couldn't imagine Luke Dalton being afraid of anything.

He said he liked to make the first move. But she wasn't going to let any macho affectations stop her now.

Without breaking eye contact, she unlocked the door and slowly pushed it open. Unblinking, she stared into his eyes, willing him to see that her determination matched her desire. She watched his expression harden with resistance.

But as she held her ground, refusing to lower her eyes, refusing to let him ignore her unspoken invitation, she saw one corner of his mouth quirk a little, then the slow hint of a smile curved his lips as his expression dissolved into resignation.

Just as slowly, without taking his eyes from her face, he stepped into her room. With a smile of triumph, she followed.

Flicking on the lamp by the door, Claire gasped in surprise to see her balcony door standing open and a shadowy figure all in black poised on the rail. The next instant the figure vanished.

Luke pushed her aside and raced after the intruder. A second later he, too, disappeared over the balcony rail.

Dashing after him, she saw him sliding down a rope hanging from the balustrade. "Luke, it's all right!" she yelled. "There's nothing here to steal!" But her words were blown back at her by the night breeze.

The dark figure could just be seen darting through the grounds below, running toward the beach. Luke, having just dropped onto the pool patio, tore after the intruder until he, too, was swallowed by the night.

Going back into the room, Claire soon discovered that it had been carefully but discreetly searched. Fortunately her passport and wallet were safe. She clutched at the diamond pendant. Luckily her only jewelry was around her neck.

She should feel upset and violated that someone had been here in her room, riffling through her belongings, but right now all she could feel was a surge of elation.

Luke was not a jewel thief!

She danced over to the phone, dizzy with relief and excitement, and dialed James's room. No answer. She hung up. No problem, she'd call him in the morning.

But where was Luke? Pacing anxiously over to the balcony, she looked down on the deserted grounds. The lanterns were turned off now and only the pool glowed an unearthly blue, suspended in the darkness. Beyond the inky mass of trees lay the pale strip of beach and the deceptively calm ocean, gleaming under the three-quarter moon.

Claire looked at her watch. It was two o'clock. He'd been gone ten minutes. She worried he might be hurt. But no, she'd already seen how well he could take care of himself.

No, her anxiety had more to do with her own selfish needs. She wanted to find out where that promising capitulation of his would lead. She just wanted to be with him.

After twenty more interminable minutes ticked by, a knock at her door had her racing to answer. She opened it to see Luke standing in the hall, his tie askew, his tuxedo jacket hanging open. In one hand he carried his shoes and a sodden pair of socks. The bottom of his pant legs were crusted with sand.

"I'm sorry, he got away."

There was something so vulnerable and endearing about the sight of him standing there in bare feet and windblown hair, with that rueful apology in his eyes that crept in and made her heart flip over.

She smiled. "It doesn't matter, nothing was taken. Come on in."

Something guarded veiled his expression and he gave her a small, regretful smile. "No, I'd better go and get out of these wet things. I just wanted to check that you were all right."

"I'm fine. But you're not going back to your room. Not yet."

8

"Don't you think you should give me the same chance that I gave you this afternoon, and let me escape?"

Her mouth curved into a catlike smile. "That *would* be the gentlemanly thing to do."

"It would be." His voice was low and soft as his gaze dropped to her mouth. Desire flared hot in his blue eyes.

A warm rush of elation welled up inside, giving her the courage to reach up, take both ends of his loosened black bow tie and pull him slowly toward her. "But I'm not a gentleman."

"Then I would say that lets me off the hook, too." He dropped the shoes, roughly pulled her into his arms and covered her mouth with his, kicking the door shut behind him.

His lips were hot and hungry. She let go of his tie and wrapped her arms around his neck, glorying in his barely restrained savagery born of impatient desire, matching her own wild, impetuous need—the kind of passion she never knew existed in her. Amazed, thrilled, even a little shocked at herself, she had to know what it was all about, drink in the experience, even if only this once. With a small moan, she molded her hips against him.

He wrenched his mouth from hers and stepped away, breathing hard, and when she would have closed the gap between them again he stopped her, capturing her face between his strong, callused hands. She could feel the frustration, even latent anger in his fingers pressing against the sides of her head, but she didn't move, just looked up into his blazing eyes. She felt no fear.

"What's the matter?"

"Do you need to ask?" He gave a sharp, derisive laugh and put her away from him. "You're driving me mad."

His hand went to the breast pocket of his jacket, then he sighed and shoved both hands into the pockets of his trousers. His face was brooding as he looked down at her. "Claire, we both know this isn't the smart thing to do. I think I'd better go."

"Why?" She sounded lethally calm, but her eyes glowed with bone-melting desire. Fear prickled his flesh and he felt himself weakening, like helpless prey as she went on. "You *want* me and I . . . I want this ache inside me to go away, and I know you can make that happen."

He ground his teeth together till it hurt. How much more of this could he stand? "I won't take that personally."

She gasped and her cheeks flared a dull pink as pain filled her eyes. "You better! I've never done anything like this, felt like this, before. Not even with Paul."

Her quiet words hit him like a sledgehammer in the ribs, making it hard to speak. "Even more reason for you to think twice about what you're doing."

"Think about it? I haven't been able to think of anything else all day." Her voice was soft, rueful, and the sexiest thing he'd ever heard. "I've never wanted anyone the way I want you."

His chest felt so tight he could barely catch his breath, barely speak. He needed an ice cube shower, right this second. Her beautiful eyes gazed up at him, heavy with desire, and his head filled with the light scent of jasmine that clung to her soft blond hair, to the downy skin of her arms. Her lush mouth parted a fraction, so incredibly inviting and irresistible. But he had to resist.

"I still think you should take a little more time, think about it..."

Stepping closer, she covered his lips with her fingertips. "Don't talk, Luke, just let it happen."

She sounded a little despairing, but the trust in her blue eyes, the feeling of her fingers against his mouth started a dangerous melting inside. Why her? Of all the women in the world why did she have to be the one to affect him like this? Because, God knows, he'd never felt anything like this before.

"I want to make love with you," she said softly.

A shudder tore through him and his whole body shook with the need to bury himself in her so deep that she'd never escape. He wanted her so badly. That's why he couldn't take her.

He gently moved her fingers away from his lips. "Claire..."

What did he want to say? He wanted to scream out the truth, tell her everything, especially before making love to her. He stopped himself abruptly. *Making love* to her? Wasn't it just sex?

Tormented, he gazed into the confusion in her eyes. And then saw them lighten with determination and laughter.

"Luke, don't force me to say that this... thing is bigger than the both of us. Even if it is."

A grim smile curved his mouth. This was insanity, this was suicide, but he couldn't help himself. He needed to take her, over and over again, until all his frustration was ground out of him.

"I guess I know when I'm licked." There was a touch of ruefulness in his heated smile.

Sheer heady devilry made her grin wickedly. "Not yet, but I'll get to it."

He laughed and she was surprised to see the flush deepen slightly on his cheeks, surprised that she could make this sophisticated, confident man self-conscious.

"But I want to take my time," she said. "I want to savor this, remember it in every detail."

Luke's smile faded, his face became serious as his fingers closed around her upper arms and he looked down into her eyes for a long moment.

"I hope I don't disappoint you," he murmured, and a shadow of his earlier resistance darkened his eyes, as if he were still fighting his need.

"Impossible." She put her hands on his waist, feeling the hard body quivering under the fine fabric of his tuxedo jacket. "I believe everyone is entitled to a night of ecstasy, and you're not going to deny me mine."

Her words erased the shadow and made his eyes gleam with wicked appreciation. He tilted his head to one side, teasing, admonishing, and very much back in control. He grabbed her wrists in his big hands and stopped their downward movement over the front of his trousers.

"There you go, being demanding again."

"What choice did I have? You'd have walked out of here if I'd let you."

"If you weren't so determined to have your way you'd have had the satisfaction of seeing that I probably wouldn't have been able to stay away for long. Now just for that, you're going to do exactly as you're told. This time, I'm calling the shots."

He released her wrists, but gently put her away from him at the same time. "First of all, don't touch me till I tell you to."

"Why not?" She smiled, already completely beyond her experience and enjoying every minute of it.

"And don't ask why not." He gave her a small, dark smile. "Just do as you're told."

His smile broadened when she just stood waiting for his next move. "Mmm...obedient...very sexy." His voice shook with suppressed laughter, his eyes glowed with excitement.

He reached out to mold the swell of her breasts in his hands, not quite touching as he traced the outline of her body down to the curve of her waist. Slowly, only a millimeter away, as the heat from his hands burned into her flesh through the silk.

He watched her face, his gaze on her lips. She licked them and saw his eyes darken. And still he didn't touch, but his hand moved up to her breast again, hovering that excruciating fraction away. Her nipples ached to be touched by him, taken into his mouth. A shudder tore through her and she closed her eyes as a slight moan escaped her.

"Open your eyes, Claire." His warm breath fanned her lips and she opened her eyes to the warm glittering desire in his, only inches away. "Good girl."

"Enjoy it while it lasts," she murmured dryly.

He chuckled deep in his throat, his smile alight with appreciation. "Come with me."

He turned and strolled unhurried to the couch, sat down and leaned back, his legs stretched out and crossed in front of him, as if settling himself to enjoy a good movie.

She slowly followed, but when she got close, he said, "That's far enough. Now," he murmured, his voice soft and lazy, "take off your clothes."

A rush of delicious excitement went coursing through her veins. Instead of being embarrassed at the idea of Luke watching her with that lazy sensual appraisal, she felt an exhilarating freedom. Hot, tingling pleasure spread over her skin as she reveled in the idea of enticing and arousing him, in the sudden assurance of her own feminine power to make him want her.

She kicked off her sandals, then reached deliberately behind her, under the short flared skirt of the dress, to hike her thumbs under the waistband of her lacy cotton briefs. And all the time she watched his face, the small smile on his lips, the narrowed eyes, his body seemingly relaxed, but she sensed that every muscle was screaming with tension.

Slowly she pulled down her briefs and stepped out of them, letting them swing from one fingertip for a moment. She saw his chest expand, taking a ragged breath, but nothing changed on his face except a fractional tightening of that waiting tension.

Letting her panties drop, she reached for the hem of her dress. As she did, he suddenly pulled in his legs and leaned forward, his elbows resting on his knees, hands clasped loosely between his spread legs. His eyes glittered with intensity.

She wanted to smash that concentration to smithereens. She wanted to make him lose control in a blinding haze of passion. With teasing slowness, she began to raise the delicate white silk, exposing her bare thighs inch by tantalizing inch.

Raising it higher, until the hem brushed over the pale triangle of curls at the apex of her thighs, she watched his eyes darken, saw the sudden flush along his cheekbones. Continuing higher, she felt the cool air on her midriff, then the moving fabric grazing over the underside of her breasts, heavy with desire. As the lifted dress covered her face she heard his quick, indrawn breath, a sound torn out of him by frustration. Her mouth curved in a small smile of satisfaction.

Then suddenly she felt his wet, hot mouth engulfing her nipple. The breath left her in a painful rush and her body went up in flames. She struggled out of the dress to see him on his knees in front of her, his dark head against her pale skin, hectic color staining his cheekbones as he hungrily suckled.

A violent gush of heat pooled between her legs and suddenly she was on the brink of orgasm. She clenched her thighs together to hold it back, and pushed his head away.

"Not yet..." she gasped, breathless. "If you keep that up it'll all be over before it begins. And you've still got your clothes on. I think it's your turn now."

He leaned back on his haunches to look up at her, his eyes hungrily appraising her. A smile of appreciation and delight spread across his face as he scanned her body.

"All right." He pulled off his tie and tossed it away.

"Wait. Not so fast. It's my turn to watch now." She headed toward the bed, giving her bottom an extra little provocative sway as she walked away from him. He reached out to trail a finger over the curve of her behind and her knees weakened.

Crawling onto the bed, she deliberately gave him a tantalizing view of her derriere and was rewarded by a groan of frustration behind her, but she could hear the appreciation and amusement there, too.

On hands and knees, she turned to look back at him, making her smile coy. He sat flopped back on his haunches in mock surrender to her tactics.

"What's the matter? Are you having a hard time?"

"Oh, you want to play dirty, do you?" His face was alive with humor and desire. He was enjoying this. "Well, that's just fine with me, but I bet I can make you come before me."

"Now what kind of bet is that?" A surge of excitement went pounding through her. They'd barely begun and she was already having more fun with this man than she ever had with anyone else. She turned and sat cross-legged on the bed, facing him.

"A good one, I'd say." Slowly, never taking his sensuous gaze off her face, he began to undo the pearl studs on his shirt.

"You're on."

As she watched, he pulled the shirt out of his pants and began to shrug out of it. Her breasts felt full and heavy, the nipples tingling and aching. His movements were unhurried, not deliberately provocative, but just the natural grace of his body was enough to arouse her, just the movement of his hard muscles under gleaming gold flesh.

Her mouth went dry. Breathlessly she said, "For a man who spends so much time behind a desk, you're in very good shape."

"Behind a de—yes...well, one must keep oneself fit."

Pain flared behind his eyes for a moment, something lonely and unhappy and it went straight to her gullible little heart. He shrugged out of his shirt and dropped it behind him. Desire knifed through her at the sight of him, his skin gleaming in the muted light.

But she couldn't forget that vulnerability she'd glimpsed, and she couldn't distance herself from her natural inclination to go to him, to offer him solace, to save him from his lonely torment. She was a sap who couldn't just take sex at face value. But she couldn't change herself, either.

Getting up slowly from the bed, she went over to kneel down in front of him and reached up for his face. For a moment he flinched back, something bleak shadowed his expression, then he let her tenderly place her hands on his cheeks.

"Don't worry," she whispered. "It's only fantasy."

"What makes you think I can afford one..."

Under her hands she felt the hard planes of his face, the bones under his skin, the masculine rasp of stubble, the tension in his jaw, in his body. More than ever she wanted to erase that tension. She wanted him to feel as free, as good, as she felt. She wanted him to feel safe.

"What makes you think you've got any choice?" she said, teasing him with a smile.

"Foolish of me, I agree." He echoed her smile and all traces of darkness vanished from his face. "Well, this is *your* fantasy, what happens next?"

"I want to kiss you all over your body." Leaning forward, she placed a kiss on his throat. "Like this..." On his Adam's apple "And this..." Her lips trailed up to graze his jaw with a series of tender kisses as she began pushing his knees apart and insinuating her body a little closer.

"Everywhere?" He sounded breathless, but with a hint of laughter.

She pressed her thigh against his crotch and felt him, hot and hard... and enormous. "Mmm—hmm... everywhere."

His eyes were closed, his lips parted as each breath came fast and ragged, his hands clenched into fists on his knees. "Then what are you waiting for? You have my permission to begin."

Again she heard the suppressed laughter in his voice. "You rat," she laughed, and once again clenched her thigh muscles together to keep back the orgasm that trembled so close to bursting free. "Even your voice is sexy, you arrogant swine." She bit his earlobe and he let out a sharp gasp.

"Feel free to abuse me some more." He chuckled.

She sucked gently on his earlobe. She could feel him beginning to tremble, a low quiver through his whole body as she delicately trailed her mouth ever closer to his, until she kissed the corner of his lips.

No, she couldn't tantalize him a second longer without tantalizing the hell out of herself.

At last, raising herself to press the length of her body against him, she kissed him full on the mouth.

The trembling became a shudder, his arms went around her and pulled her tight against him. With a groan, he took her mouth in a hard, almost savage kiss that she returned with equal ferocity.

Through the fine wool of his pants she could feel him hard and hot and pressed against her. Working her hands between them, she fumbled with the button. His hand slid down her body with a delicious abrasion to knead her bottom with a hard, almost painful urgency that felt incredibly good.

Without stopping the kiss he managed to help her fumbling efforts and soon the rest of his clothing was out of the way.

He got to his feet in one lithe movement, picked her up as if she weighed nothing, and carried her over to the bed and laid her down. Standing above her for a moment, he was so perfect, so beautiful—hard and ready for her.

"Now, do you promise to respect me in the morning?" His mouth curved into that wolfish smile that made her tingle right down to her toes.

"I promise." And she couldn't wait another moment longer. "And by the way, the bet's off."

"Thank God for that," he muttered under his breath, low and caressing as he lowered himself down beside her. Rolling on top, he nestled his hips between her legs and she wrapped them around him, aching to get closer, to feel him where she wanted him.

Raised on his elbows, Luke gazed down at her. "So soon?"

She nodded. "If you don't mind."

"I guess we'll have to leave the foreplay for next time."

"I thought we already had it . . ." She gasped as he entered her.

"Heavens, no, that was only the beginning," he said on a breathless laugh as he buried himself deep within her.

He lay still for a moment, looking down at her, and something dark and serious clouded his eyes again. "You're so beautiful. I never knew I could want someone so much." With one trembling hand, he smoothed the hair back off her forehead and gently traced over the line of her jaw.

For a man who could be so tough, his touch was the most tender thing she'd ever felt, the reverence of it brought tears to her eyes. It made her want to give of her deepest self, to let him in, not just into her body, but into her soul.

She reached up and pulled his head down to her. Even if only for this once, she wanted to make this as special for him as it was turning out to be for her. She'd been expecting just a physical union, but she was feeling so much more than she'd ever anticipated. She wanted to absorb him, be absorbed by him.

Her tongue slipped into his mouth, exploring the wet warmth, reveling in the taste of him. With a groan, he kissed her back and began to move inside her. The long, slow strokes rapidly became faster and harder.

She wrapped her legs more tightly around him, moving with him, opening herself more completely to his thrusts. Running her hands obsessively over his back, she caressed and squeezed, from the nape of his neck down to the powerful muscles contracting in his buttocks. Gasping for breath, she felt herself drowning in sensation, felt the simmering volcano building inside her until she thought she'd die from pleasure.

His hot mouth was everywhere; his teeth grazing her shoulder, his hands squeezing her arms, until at last he buried his face in the curve of her neck and finally shuddered and gasped helplessly in his release.

But he kept moving, with slow, hot pulses that drove her closer to the brink. "Oh, Luke, please don't stop now."

"Not a chance." His voice was ragged. "I want you to feel like I do right now. I want you to come all over me."

Orgasm hit her like a tidal wave as he moved with her, speeding up again, driving her back up to the peak while she could only cling to him and gasp wordless cries of pleasure.

Now she understood what it was all about. The mindless force of nature that could drive men and women to despair and excess. How you could lose your mind, lose *yourself* in something this overwhelming, and count the world well lost?

HE CAME BACK silently into the bedroom and looked down at Claire's sleeping form. The weak lamplight filtered in from the sitting area to gleam on her golden hair spread over the pillow. Covered only by the thin sheet that molded her delicious slender curves, she lay with her cheek resting on one hand, asleep and defenseless.

A surge of tender protectiveness tightened his throat, making him feel like a complete bastard for what he'd been doing for the past ten minutes.

At the beginning he'd known his only hope for getting through this night had been to reduce the encounter to the level of a sex game, but it had backfired on him in the most appalling, unexpected way. And it served him right.

But what about Claire? He deliberately shoved that question out of his mind; he didn't want to answer it.

With silent efficiency he searched the closet beside the bathroom, grimly trying to repress the feelings of self-disgust and concentrate on the job at hand. Unfortunately Nikki hadn't finished, so he had to take up where she'd left off.

But, thank God, he hadn't found anything yet. Maybe he was a coward, but he didn't want to find anything tonight.

Only the dresser left. He swiftly went through the drawers, starting at the bottom, and was just closing the top drawer when he heard a husky murmur.

"Hi."

He turned to see Claire sitting up with a sleepy smile, her hair tousled around her head.

"What are you looking for?"

There was nothing accusatory in her question, but he felt guilt knifing through him. "Some aspirins. I'm getting a bit of a headache."

She shook her head. "I don't have any."

Then her smile became warm and sweetly, innocently, provocative. She'd given of herself so generously, so unreservedly. Once again he felt anger burning inside him. *Why* did she have to be who she was? Suddenly it hit him that he was so tired of all the deceit, and it wasn't over yet, not by a long shot. The damn call couldn't come soon enough for him.

"But if you come back to bed," she continued playfully, "I'll see what I can do about getting rid of your headache."

He shouldn't go back to her, he should leave right now. But, God help him, he couldn't. He moved slowly to the bed and sat down beside her. This was real. The way she made him feel was unlike anything he'd ever experienced before. The thought left him terrified. Why? Why did it have to be her?

Claire turned toward him with a smile and put her arm on his shoulder, her fingers twirling in the hair at the nape of his neck, sending little shivers to race across his skin.

"What's the matter? Why are you so tense?" she murmured.

He looked at her consideringly for a moment. He knew what he wanted, what he needed to do right now. To forget all about the other business, just for tonight, to put it out of his head and pretend they were two different people. "Why do you think?"

She smiled and it was his undoing. "Oh, I see. Well, then, what are you going to do about it?"

"I'll show you." He laid her down on the pillows. She went to put her arms around him, but he took her hands one at a time and wrapped her fingers around the wicker headboard. If she touched him at all, it would be game over. He was like a teenager, unable to control his rampant need. "You mustn't move your hands from this position."

Her eyes gleamed with mischievous amusement, but she kept her face solemn as he hovered above her, kneeling between her slightly parted legs.

He lowered his head to kiss her, slowly, gently allowing his tongue to explore her warm, delicious mouth, then grazed his lips down her neck, over the rising curve of her breast. Her skin tasted sweet, soft against his lips. Could he ever get enough of her?

If he had a woman like her in his home, in his bed, he'd never want to do anything but this. And no doubt make a complete ass of himself, to boot.

The more he got, the more he seemed to crave. Pressing kisses around her nipple, he teased the little bud into a tight peak before finally taking it into his mouth. Already he was so hard, so desperate for her.

She moaned and her hands came down to hold his head, threading her fingers through his hair. It cost him, but he deliberately stopped and looked up at her flushed face.

He loved seeing the effect he had on her, watching her arousal made him even harder. He wanted to prolong his own desire, that way when the moment of release came he might, finally, be satisfied.

Her fingers kneaded his scalp and he gently shook his head and smiled. "Uh-uh, remember? Hands."

With a groan of frustration, she let go and moved her hands back to grasp the headboard again, but he could also see the devilish sparkle of enjoyment in her bright eyes. She was spirited and daring; in so many ways the perfect woman for him.

"Good girl."

He let his frustrated gaze roam over her body beneath him, over the curves of her breasts. Her fair skin had a peachy blush from the sun, her nipples pink and tempting and so tasty.

Inching his way down, he placed his lips against her flesh and felt her stomach muscles rippling beneath the touch of his mouth. The heady taste of her sent sharp arrows of arousal to his throbbing loins, but what he really needed was still waiting.

When he dipped his tongue into the indent of her navel, she twisted her body sinuously against him and let out a breathless little moan. He looked up to see her hanging tightly on to the headboard, her eyes closed in her flushed face and her head thrown back. The sight sent a fresh surge of arousal roaring through his body, making him so hard it was painful.

He dipped his head quickly, his mouth finding what he'd been waiting for for so long.

As soon as he tasted her dusky sweetness it was all over. With her arching against his mouth, with her low, ecstatic moan of pleasure filling his ears, he couldn't stop himself, he came.

CLAIRE AWOKE filled with lazy contentment. She stretched and wriggled, her body throbbing and slightly aching and incredibly satisfied. Then she thought of Luke, and the hunger began all over again. She turned over to reach for him and found the other side of the bed empty.

A disappointed, hollow feeling raced through her. Raising herself up on one elbow, she saw the indentation of his head on the pillow and leaned down to put her face against it, breathing in the lingering scent of him.

With a sigh, she sat up and pushed the hair off her face. So that was that. She'd hoped he'd stay until the morning, but perhaps he'd deliberately left before she woke. There was no reason to feel bereft. It had been a fantasy evening come true and she had to enjoy the moment and not pine now that it was over. She refused to let herself feel melancholy.

Swinging her feet to the floor, she noticed a folded sheet of hotel stationery on the bedside table. She snatched it up eagerly.

Good morning, Claire, darling,
Didn't want to wake you, although the temptation was almost irresistible. Last night only whetted my appetite. I want more. Meet me for lunch. Your room, noon. Don't be late, you're the starter course.

"Bossy devil," she murmured, but a quiver of sensual anticipation made her mouth curve in a wicked smile and she felt happier than she'd felt in a long, long time as she headed for the shower.

Under the fine, hot spray she closed her eyes and relived the intoxicating, tempestuous night they had shared. She should be exhausted from lack of sleep, but she felt exhilarated and energized, and looking forward to seeing him again. Luke had been...incredible, everything a fantasy lover should be, except for those moments when she'd sensed something pained and tormented in him.

She'd sensed his loneliness. Was he a lonely man? Was that why he was vacationing alone? Or had he just broken up with his girlfriend and was just nursing a broken heart? On the rebound, like he'd accused her of being.

Suddenly a much more unwelcome reason hit her and she cursed herself for a fool for not thinking of it before. Could he be married? Was that why she sensed the guilt, the torment? As she stepped out and wrapped herself in the fluffy hotel towel, she shivered. The very real possibility gave her a cold chill.

Because if he was married, then even just once wasn't right. She might rail against her mother's old-fashioned values, but she couldn't shrug off something like that.

But, no, he just didn't seem like the type of man who'd sneak around, cheating on someone behind her back. But she didn't know him, and pangs of guilt over an infidelity would certainly explain his initial reluctance. Before she allowed this to go any further she'd have to put her doubts at rest, because she *did* want to see him again.

After toweling off, she slipped on her robe and was just emerging from the bathroom when the phone began to ring. She ran to answer it.

"Good morning, darling."

Her shoulders sagged, a little deflated to hear her father's voice. "Oh...hi, Dad."

"Try to contain your excitement."

The droll inflection in his caustic brogue made her smile. "Sorry, I was expecting someone else."

"Hmm..." The one syllable held a tinge of impatience and scorn. "Well, put that someone else out of your mind for a little while, I have a job for you."

9

HE CAME straight to the point. "I want you to go down to the Frangipani Café on the mezzanine and get yourself breakfast from the buffet. You'll notice a man sitting at a table for two overlooking the lobby. He's wearing a bright blue Hawaiian shirt. He's tall, with short, dark hair and looks to be in his mid-thirties. His name is Herb Whittaker. I'd like you to go down and make sure he doesn't come near his room. Give me two hours."

Her stomach muscles tightened. "Is he the courier?"

"There's every possibility that he could be." Her father's voice was brisk and businesslike. "Now wish me luck." He sounded as if he was about to hang up.

"Wait a minute!" she said desperately.

"I can't talk and you don't have time. Get there as quick as you can."

The line went dead and Claire stood for a moment staring at the phone. What about lunch with Luke?

A glance at her watch told her it was eight o'clock. Okay, she'd have time. But she hadn't even had a chance to tell James about the intruder last night—that Luke couldn't possibly be the jewel thief. Oh, well, she'd tell him later.

Quickly throwing on a pair of white shorts and a pale pink tank top, she ran a comb through her hair and put on a dash of lipstick. She wouldn't bother with makeup, especially in the heat. Besides, she'd better be quick in case the man finished his breakfast and left.

The café was bright and sunny and already quite busy as she hurried in and then forced herself to slow down and act casual. Walking past the huge arrangement of frangipani blossoms scenting the air, she ignored the sign that asked guests to wait to be seated. She intended to choose her own seat.

A sumptuous buffet was laid out in the center of the long room, which was filled with the lively babble of voices and the clatter of cutlery. Claire sauntered over to the tables laden with a profusion of fruit, cereal, eggs and pastries—any kind of breakfast one might wish for. But her mind wasn't on food as she rapidly scanned the room.

There he was. It had to be him, sitting by the railing overlooking the lobby and reading a newspaper. He was the only lone man who fit the description. Actually he was quite attractive, tall and handsome.

Claire's stomach gave a flip of anxiety. What did she know about playing the femme fatale? Heaven knows, this man had better be the one. Then she could get her task over and done with and enjoy the short time she had left with Luke.

That thought gave her the nerve she needed. Afraid to take her eyes off her prey, Claire picked up a plate and began inattentively helping herself from the buffet. The question was, how on earth could she keep him busy for two hours? She'd have to engage him in conversation.

With what she hoped looked like casual ease, she strolled over and seated herself with aplomb at the table next to his. In a flash of inspiration, she surreptitiously palmed the salt shaker and dropped it under her chair. The loud clatter it made on the polished teak floor sounded ear-splitting. Claire winced, already she was making a mess of this.

In an instant a smiling waiter was at her elbow, handing it back to her. Gritting her teeth, she smiled back insincerely. So much for that ploy. She definitely wasn't cut out for undercover work. Luckily her neighbor didn't even glance up from his paper.

This time she'd be a little smarter. Removing the small pepper mill from the table, she dropped it carefully in her lap. Leaning over toward the dark-haired man, she planted a brilliant smile on her face and came as close to batting her lashes as she could stomach.

"Excuse me, could you please pass the pepper? I don't seem to have any."

The man idly glanced at her over the top of his paper, then quickly put it down on the table with comic alacrity. She seemed to have an effect on some men, but she didn't usually exploit it so shamelessly.

"Why, certainly." Eagerly, he handed over his pepper mill.

She took it, then looked down at her plate and found to her horror that it was piled with fruit salad. Looking up at him again, she saw puzzled bemusement on his face as he too stared at her breakfast.

"People think I'm mad, but I love pepper on fruit," she said airily, and ground a liberal amount over her plate. "You should try it sometime, it's delicious." She ate a spoonful and tried not to grimace as the fire spread through her mouth.

He smiled and shook his head. "No, thanks, I'll take your word for it."

Instead of going back to his paper, the man just sat and watched her in fascination. With a forced smile of enjoyment, she took another mouthful. She was going to choke this stuff down if it killed her. Better he think that she had strange tastes, than suspect her of deliberately keeping him busy while his room was being searched.

On the third mouthful of peppered fruit her eyes began to water. *Say something to him, you fool!* After all, she'd certainly managed to get his attention.

Blinking back the moisture, she took a quick sip of ice water to douse the fire in her mouth, then smiled at him. "This is a lovely place, isn't it?" She wanted to wince at how phony she sounded—too bright, too forced.

He nodded, still smiling. "Yes, very."

"Are you here alone, Mr.—" She stopped herself just in time. *Idiot*! She'd almost blurted out his name!

"Whittaker, Herb Whittaker." To her relief he took her sudden pause as an invitation to introduce himself. "And I'm here with a friend."

"Oh."

"We came to fish, but he met someone last night who obviously interested him a lot more," he said quickly, as if eager to reassure her that his friend wasn't a woman. "Can't say I blame him, she's a lovely lady," he added with a shy diffidence she would normally have found endearing.

"Where are you from, Herb?"

"Toledo, Ohio. I have a small general contracting business there. How about you?"

"Toronto, Canada." Why was it when people met on holiday the first thing they mentioned after their name was where they came from and what they did? Everybody except Luke, that is.

But just as quickly she put Luke out of her mind. She had a job to do, and so far she'd made too many idiotic mistakes.

Talking to Herb turned out to be surprisingly easy. If this man was an underworld courier, she was Nancy Drew! But then again, appearances weren't everything. After all, what about James? Looking at him, who would ever suspect what *he* was doing here? But Herb seemed like a nice man, too pleasant and self-deprecating for the demands of the criminal world.

In no time at all he was bringing his coffee over to her table and sitting down in the chair opposite hers. Almost sure that he was the wrong man, she began to relax a little, carefully concealing the extra pepper mill under her crumpled napkin. This Mata Hari stuff wasn't so hard after all. And when it was over she'd be seeing Luke again.

LUKE KNOCKED on her door, determined to smother the ridiculous feelings of anger and betrayal threatening to tear him apart. So what if he'd seen her happily eating breakfast with another man? She could do what she wanted.

She opened the door, her face breaking into a smile. "Hello." She took his hand and pulled him into her room. "You're late, I thought you weren't coming."

"I didn't think it would matter to you if I were a little late." He'd had to force himself to come, telling himself it would be unprofessional to let these ridiculous personal feelings of his get in the way.

"Of course it matters to me." She put her arms around him, pressing herself against him.

He hardened himself against the urge to pull her closer. He put her away from him; he had to fight this compulsion to let himself drown in his need for her, to forget about everything. How could she stand there looking so innocent? Hadn't he just seen her talking, laughing, enjoying herself with another man?

"Luke, is something wrong?" her soft voice trailed off as she searched his face, concern darkening her eyes.

He didn't want to see that concern. He wanted to keep the picture of her smiling up at that man in the forefront of his mind. "No, nothing is wrong." He paused, determined not to mention that he'd followed her down to the restaurant. "Who was that man you were talking to at breakfast?"

Damn it! Why was he behaving like this?

She gave him a blank look. "What man? Oh, Herb Whittaker."

"Yes, Herb Whittaker." He tried to control his voice and the anger he felt building up inside.

"Just a nice man I met at breakfast. Why didn't you come over, why didn't you join us? I didn't see you downstairs."

"That's not surprising, you two looked pretty cozy together." He clenched his jaw until it hurt.

Pain and confusion filled her eyes. "Don't be silly, we were only talking."

So, now he was being silly. He didn't even want to think about the fact that she was right.

He forced himself to saunter into the room past her, feigning a casualness that couldn't be further from the way he felt inside. A seething mass of contradictory emotions was pulling him apart.

"Nevertheless, I didn't want to intrude." *Balls*. He'd wanted to walk up and smash the guy's face in.

The thought made his head reel. In spite of his profession, he wasn't a violent man. He'd laugh if it weren't so pathetic.

"Intrude! Luke, don't tell me you were jealous?" Her blue eyes widened as she stared at him, incredulous.

It hit him like a sledgehammer. Oh, my God, that's exactly what he was—jealous.

"Don't be ridiculous," he muttered, and turned away from her, feeling like a complete fool.

She came around in front of him and looked up into his face. "You are! You're jealous." She looked astonished, but pleased.

"And I suppose that makes you happy."

"Not if it makes you so miserable."

The genuine caring in her eyes made him feel unbearably bleak. It was all he could do not to take her in his arms.

Damn, he was in way over his head. It wasn't just sex, she made him feel things he'd never felt before. If she were any other woman he'd be in danger of falling in love with her. But that could never happen.

He mustn't confuse love with the explosive chemistry between them that went light-years beyond anything he'd ever known. Because he knew damn well who she was, and what she was up to! But that hadn't stopped him from acting like a prize idiot.

"Speaking of being miserable, there's something else bothering you." She paused for a moment. "Luke, are you married?"

For a moment he gave her a blank look, then suddenly expelled his breath in a low, husky chuckle. That rich, black velvet sound that tingled down her spine and made her feel warm all over.

He tilted his head to one side with a bright smile in his wolf eyes. "Now what woman in her right mind would marry a man like me?"

She couldn't help smiling back. That was one load off her mind. "And what kind of man are you?"

"Difficult. I have no patience, I'm dictatorial..."

"You're not kidding."

"...And I like my freedom," he continued, raising an eyebrow at her heartfelt agreement.

"So far you sound just like Ja—" She stopped short, cursing herself for being so unwary. She didn't want to come as close to James as even mentioning his name. But naturally he'd noticed.

"Just like who?"

"My father." She hurried on. "Anyway, you were telling me why you'd be such a rotten candidate for marriage. So far you sound like a lot of other men—" she smiled "—who *are* married."

"Then there's my job. I'm never home."

It was becoming an effort to keep her mind on their conversation, when her attention was straying to his hard, tempting mouth. "But you're a banker."

He hesitated for an infinitesimal moment. "A banker who travels a lot."

"Are you a good banker?"

"Reasonably good."

"If you bank the way you make love, then you must be very successful."

At that he threw back his head and laughed. Yet she was amused to see a slight tinge of red along his cheekbones.

"Thank you." Then his smile turned rueful. He took a deep breath and let it out again, looking her straight in the eyes, and she could see he was disturbed. "The reason I acted like such an idiot when I came in was because I saw you with that guy in the restaurant and I didn't like it."

Something soared inside her as she met the hunger burning in his eyes, saw the tension in his face, in his hard mouth.

"You really were jealous?"

"Okay, I was jealous. Are you satisfied?" he said, his jaw tense, his voice quiet but brimming with self-derision. "Seeing you with the guy made me want to break his neck."

"We were only talking," she said faintly.

Something was happening here, something beyond the fantasy sexual adventure. Something scary. This was a place she'd never been before.

"I still didn't like it," Luke repeated quietly, his jaw so tense that it made the cleft in his chin even more pronounced.

Without even really completely understanding it, Claire felt overwhelmed by a wave of tenderness for him, by the desire to soothe him. Having these kinds of feelings for a man just passing through her life could be potentially devastating. Was she strong enough to survive this?

Taking a step toward him, she put a hand on his arm and felt his muscles immediately contract at her touch. The instantaneous response sent a little zing of electricity buzzing through her.

"I want you." She could hear the burgeoning hunger in her own soft, throaty voice. "When I'm near you I feel like my body's on fire. No one has ever made me feel like this before, and I may never feel this way again. I don't want Whittaker, I want you."

What was the point in lying? She stepped closer and felt a shudder pass through his body.

"Claire." His hands tightened on her forearms and she was afraid he would push her away.

She raised a hand to caress his face, to trace his tense jaw until she allowed a finger to slide into the cleft in his chin, her voice soft and provocative. "How do you shave here?"

"Very carefully," he answered through gritted teeth, and grabbed her wrist in a hard grip to hold her hand away from him.

What was he afraid of? What was holding him back? But now at least she knew her power over him. Moving close, she wrenched her hand out of his grip and pressed herself against him, putting her arms around his neck.

"You did promise me lunch," she whispered against his mouth.

With a small groan of capitulation, his arms went around her, gathering her to him. His lips were hard and demanding on hers, like a man starved, and she reveled in his urgent hunger.

It felt as if she'd been away from him for months, not just a few hours. Already she was addicted to the taste of his mouth, the feel of his hardness against her. Her body knew him, fitting into his familiarly as she melted against him, thrilling to the feverish touch of his hands, stroking everywhere, caressing, sliding down over her back to squeeze her buttocks.

"So what did you feel like having for lunch?" he breathed against her mouth, and roughly pulled the tank top free of her shorts. Then his hands were on her bare flesh, sliding up over her rib cage until his thumbs grazed the tight peaks of her nipples and set off a shocking, searing explosion of pleasure.

With a gasp, she pressed closer, feeling him hard and aroused against her. "More of this, if you don't mind," she said breathlessly.

"I don't mind at all." He barely got out the distracted words as he pulled her top up all the way, baring her breasts.

She looked down at his long, tanned fingers cupping and stroking her pale flesh, making goose bumps appear on her skin. She sucked in her breath as his hands moved over her, the callused palms that caused a torrent of excruciating desire through her until she couldn't stand it a second longer.

She grabbed his hands and pulled them away, burying her face in his palms, and began to press her lips to the rough, hard flesh. Lifting her head, she looked down wonderingly and stroked the rough, hard calluses at the base of his fingers. "For a man who pushes paper, you sure have rough hands."

"I'm sorry. Did I hurt you?"

"On the contrary, no other hands have ever made me feel so good. When you touch me, I could almost purr with sheer bliss."

Paul's hands had been so soft, in retrospect they seemed almost effeminate. Now she couldn't imagine any other man but Luke touching her.

Once again she put his hands against her breasts and looked at him. In one movement he wrapped his arms around her waist and lifted her until his hot mouth surrounded one taut, aching peak.

Urgently she wrapped her legs around his hips, pressing closer until she could feel his hardness against her, where she wanted it to be, where it felt so good.

His mouth teased and tormented her, sending shuddering jolts of heat straight to the spot where she pressed against him. With a slow, hard rhythm she began moving her hips, grinding herself against his erection. He groaned deep in his throat and pulled on her nipple with a powerful suckling that made her gasp his name.

Tangling her hands in his thick, dark hair, she closed her eyes, giving herself up to the flood of hot, liquid sensation, the familiar building unbearable tension, even through the layers of clothing. Amazement filled her. It was actually going to happen, right now, without even getting undressed. She gasped in unison with his breathing, with the responding movement of his hips against hers, with the rhythm of his hot, wet suckling.

The sharp ring of the phone broke the gasping, breathy silence.

"No," Luke groaned in anguish against her breast. "Damn it, not now."

"I'm not going to answer." She could barely speak coherently. "Please don't stop."

He gave a guttural moan as her movements became more urgent. "No fear of that." He matched her frantic rhythm.

Luke shuddered against her as the phone went on ringing relentlessly in the background, but she didn't care. Right now the whole world was between her thighs.

The jangling noise stopped and all that could be heard was their low moans and soft gasps as they undulated more rapidly against each other.

And then he tensed. A second later he was shuddering as his release swept over him. That same moment she felt the orgasm slamming into her with an intensity that left her gasping and clinging on to him, her shorts getting wetter and wetter.

At last they both went still, his arms tight around her like iron bands so that she could barely breathe. Utterly, ecstatically sated, she allowed herself to sag against him, feeling little ebbing pulses of release shuddering through her.

Trembling from the strain, Luke slowly lowered her to her feet, but kept her tightly wrapped in his arms. He chuckled breathlessly against her lips. "That has to be a first for me."

"Me, too." She managed a shaky laugh.

His arms still around her, he began moving backward toward the bed. "If I don't sit down, I'm going to fall down."

He plonked down on the bed, pulling her down beside him.

The shrill ring of the phone sounded again. It could only be James. She groaned. Right now she didn't want to be bothered with all that cloak-and-dagger stuff, but if she didn't answer he'd just keep calling.

Reluctantly, Claire pulled away from Luke's warm embrace and sat up. "I'll only be a moment."

She smiled down at him apologetically and suddenly felt a little shy at the warmth and intimacy glowing in his eyes as he lay there, watching her.

Turning to the bedside table, she picked up the phone. "Hello?"

"What the hell kept you?"

She was still too filled with blissful satisfaction to get annoyed at James's peremptory question. "I was busy."

"With Dalton?"

"Yes." She felt herself blush at the thought of her father knowing just exactly what kept them so busy.

"Well, get rid of him. I have another job for you."

It felt like someone had dumped her in ice water. "Now!" she wailed in disbelief.

"Yes, now."

"But..."

"Don't argue with me, Claire. This is important. His name is Klaus Voorhees. He's just come down to the pool. I'll meet you down here and point him out to you."

"Now?" Could he possibly have picked a worse time?

"Yes," he repeated impatiently. "*Now*." And then he hung up.

She slowly put down the receiver and turned to find Luke lying back, watching her, his hands laced behind his head.

She licked her lips, painfully aware of how coldly abrupt this would look to him. "I'm sorry, I have to go."

"Where?" He raised an eyebrow in surprise.

"That was a phone call from work. I have to go downstairs and wait for a fax." It was amazing how smoothly the lie came to her. But as Luke sat up she found it impossible to look him in the eye. She got to her feet and headed for the bathroom. "It's this Pfeiffer estate I'm handling," she said over her shoulder. "It's been no end of trouble, and anyway, can we meet later? Can we meet for dinner?"

"Do you expect it to take all afternoon?" His voice reached her in the bathroom as she slipped off her damp shorts.

"At least." As she stepped out of her underwear she gasped at the unexpected touch of his hands on her bare bottom, sliding between her legs to caress her where she still burned.

"Eight, then?" he murmured from behind her as his fingers continued to stroke and tease her.

"Yes... eight," she breathed, closing her eyes at the spiraling rush of sensation.

She felt his mouth nuzzling at the corner of her lips, his hot breath mingling with hers. "Do you really have to go?"

So soon and yet his fingers were bringing her again to the brink of destruction.

She deliberately opened her eyes and moved away. "Yes, I really do." Trying not to look at him, she noticed that he was as ready for more as she. Resisting that clutching need was almost more than she was capable of.

Luke sighed. "All right. If you really have to." He placed a soft, possessive kiss on her lips. "I'll see you later," he promised, and walked out of the room. A moment later she heard the soft click of the room door closing.

Claire turned to stare at the woman in the mirror. Was that her? Her hair a tawny mane tumbled around her face, her lips rosy and slightly swollen from being thoroughly kissed, her face still flushed with passion—she looked like a woman who had been thoroughly made love to, she thought with smug satisfaction.

Well, she had better get that look off her face before she got downstairs or James's sharp eyes would catch it.

She took a two-minute shower and made it ice cold, determined to ruthlessly quell that feverish hunger she couldn't seem to sate, the throbbing heat she could still feel pulsing through her veins.

Pulling on her white bathing suit, she scrambled into a peach tank dress, slipped on her sandals and hurried out the door and downstairs.

At poolside she hovered uncertainly, seeing no sign of James anywhere. Not knowing what else to do, she headed for the hibiscus-shrouded cabana and took a towel from the attendant.

A few people splashed in the pool, but most were lounging around on deck chairs, taking the sun or reading under gaily striped umbrellas, but still no James.

"You're looking in the wrong place," a familiar voice said softly in her ear. "Look up."

Resisting the urge to turn and acknowledge her father, she followed his instructions. At the closer end of the pool a man was ascending the ladder to the high diving board. He strutted to the end, obviously aware that many pairs of eyes were now on him.

She had to admit he was quite striking—tall, dark, and with the kind of tanned, sculpted body any man would envy, and many women would lust after. And he knew it, too. "Oh, no. Not him."

"What's the matter?"

Claire heaved a sigh. "This guy's going to be fun. It's obvious he thinks he's God's gift."

"You're right, but that should only make your job easier," James said softly from behind her. "Give me two hours."

"Thanks a lot," she said sarcastically, watching suspect number two pause at the end of the diving board and nonchalantly pose for effect, knowing he was the focus of attention. "I have a feeling he's not going to be as easy to manage as poor Herb."

After a moment of silence behind her she turned to find James already gone. A muted splash and a smattering of applause made her turn back. Oh, darn, and after all that fancy build-up she'd missed the grand dive.

Taking a seat under an umbrella-shaded table, she watched as he swam to the side and climbed up the ladder to repeat the performance. He was very good-looking, she had to admit, but the self-satisfied smirk on his face totally turned her off. When she thought of Luke's unconscious sensuality, where every little movement could thrill her so unbearably, this man paled into insignificance.

Oh, well, as long as he showed no signs of leaving, she didn't even have to approach him. She settled down on a deck chair to watch the performance and soak up a little sun.

But only fifteen minutes later he climbed out of the water and picked up a towel. After carelessly drying off his chest and arms, he slung the towel around his neck and gave every sign of walking away.

Without even thinking, she lunged out of the chair and quickly covered the distance between them.

"Hi!" She stopped in front of him, not even wanting to think how brazen she must look. "That was an incredible dive! What kind of a dive was that?"

Part of her was stunned at the way she could just glibly babble on and bat her lashes for all she was worth. This must be called "getting in touch with your inner bimbo."

He bared his perfect teeth and smiled with a flash of predatory interest, his accent vaguely European. "A double gainer with a half twist back spin."

"Wow! And you performed it magnificently," she gushed. At this rate she'd be auditioning for game shows pretty soon.

"Why, thank you." His grin gleamed, positively sharklike, in his swarthy face.

Like Herb Whittaker, he was tall and dark. There was a superficial resemblance between them, a resemblance that ended with one look into those sharp, rapacious eyes. This man was a very different animal.

His hooded hawk's eyes half closed as he literally preened himself on her admiration. She suppressed a shudder.

"You're not leaving already, are you?" she simpered, smiling up at him and shading her eyes from the sun with her hand.

She noticed his gaze slide to her breasts and stay there. "I could be persuaded to stay."

I'm sure you could, Amoeba Man. "That would be lovely. Perhaps you can do your dive for me again." This could be a way out, if she could get the big ape to perform for her.

And perform he did, at least for a while, showing off his repertoire of complicated and superbly executed dives. But all too soon he emerged from the pool again and sank down at the round wrought-iron table, in the padded lounge chair beside hers.

"Here, have a banana." She reached into the complimentary fruit bowl sitting in the middle of the table and handed him one.

He took it from her and dropped it on the glass tabletop. "I'll have it later." Then he turned his full attention on her. "So, what's your name, lovely lady?"

His smarmy smile was bad enough, but then he moved his chair around closer, right next to hers, leaned his elbow on the table and smiled into her eyes.

She had to fight the urge to strain away from him. There was something hard, almost cruel, about the set of his full mouth, and his eyes raked over her in a way that made her feel unclean. She would never, ever, want to be alone with this man.

"Claire." With an effort, she put on her vacuous smile. "My name is Claire."

"So tell me, Claire, would you like to come upstairs to my room with me?"

She sucked in her breath. *The pig.* If she said no, he likely wouldn't waste another moment on her.

"What for?" The smile felt pinned to her face as she tried to make her expression as ingenuous as possible.

He looked a little taken aback and jerked his head knowingly. "You know."

She shook her head. "No. No, I don't." Opening her eyes even wider, she prayed he would buy her act.

His brow furrowed with a hint of doubt, but he was clearly surprised that a woman could have reached her age and be so totally clueless. To her disgust, she also detected more than a little lascivious delight to find such a novelty.

Surreptitiously, she snuck a look at her watch. Oh, God, another hour left to go of this torture. Could she string him along for another sixty minutes?

His voice became low and oily with suggestiveness. "I thought maybe we could go up to my room and we could spend the afternoon making love."

"Making love?" She tried to sound shocked and confused at the same time. "But we don't even know each other!"

"No, that's what makes it even more fun. Love with the perfect stranger. And I *am* the perfect stranger." His smile was all teeth and half-closed eyes.

Claire lowered her gaze modestly, torn between the urge to burst out laughing or throw up. "Oh, I don't know, it just seems so . . . so wicked. I don't know anything about you."

"My name is Klaus." He seemed to be accentuating the European accent now, maybe he thought it made him sexy.

"Is that German?"

"Half." He leaned a little closer and trailed a finger along the line of her jaw. His warm breath fanned her face and she shivered, unable to contain her revulsion.

"And what's the other half?" As she tried to strain away, his arm came around her shoulder, pulling her inexorably closer.

"Dutch." His hot, dry lips grazed her jawline where his finger had been.

At that moment she saw Luke standing on the other side of the pool. Even from a distance she could see his face harden with cold, bleak anger that stiffened every line of his body. Either she was having really lousy luck, or Luke was following her.

Klaus was continuing. "My father was Dutch."

As she pulled away from Klaus, she saw Luke's mouth twist in contempt. She jumped to her feet.

"Where are you going?" he demanded.

"I'm sorry, I have to leave."

"So suddenly? We were just getting to know each other."

"Sorry, I—I have to go. Maybe I'll see you later." There was another forty-five minutes left, but she couldn't stand this man pawing her one more minute, and she couldn't let Luke walk away without explaining, somehow.

Luke had already disappeared into the shrubbery and she dashed after him in the same direction.

Following him down the flagstone path, she nearly bumped into James. He gave a brief shake of his head as he passed her by. Obviously he hadn't found anything.

But at this moment, except for the fact that James was safe from discovery, none of that mattered. All she cared about was finding Luke, explaining, taking away the pain and anger she'd seen on his face.

Why should it matter so much to her? Just watching Luke walk away, a man she'd known for only a few days, had hurt her more than Paul's callous desertion after three years together. Why? What was happening to her?

Whatever it was, it had gone well beyond a physical attraction. But how could that have happened in such a short span of time with a man who was still a complete mystery to her? She was in danger of doing it again, giving her heart too quickly, too easily.

But she ruthlessly pushed the thought aside. She didn't want to analyze this, she wanted to let it happen, go for the experience. And if it led to sadness, as the parting inevitably would, that was what it would cost her, but she was willing to pay it and it would be worth the price. Besides, she'd weathered other disappointments, other hurts, and she'd bounced back. How deep could *these* feelings go?

She didn't know, because she didn't understand them. But right now she just wanted to be with Luke.

10

OUTSIDE THE DOOR of his room she stopped and dragged in a nervous breath. What if he told her to go away? Firming her shoulders, along with her resolve, she knocked at the door. Whatever happened, she'd deal with it.

A moment later the door swung abruptly open and Luke stood scowling down at her.

"You have to let me explain..." But she didn't get any further as he reached out, grabbed her wrist and yanked her into the room.

Slamming the door closed and pulling her roughly into his arms in one movement, he kissed her hard and long. Dazedly, joyfully, she responded.

Finally he pulled away from her and she gasped breathlessly, "I wasn't kissing that man, he was kissing me."

"I know, but..."

"But you didn't like it," she murmured with a smile as she nuzzled against his mouth. "I could give you the whole story, but I don't want to waste any more time on that octopus in bathing trunks."

"Thank God for that!" His voice was deep and vibrant with desire as he effortlessly swung her up into his arms and strode over to the bed.

WAKING to the sound of the shower, Claire sat up and pulled her knees to her chest, rocking back and forth in satiated contentment. If she were a cat she'd be purring.

Scanning the room, she smiled at the sight of Luke's discarded clothes strewn over the floor, at his watch lying on the bedside table.

She'd never been in his room before, except for that quick escape from his balcony. The layout was exactly like hers, with tropical wicker furniture upholstered in blues and greens where hers were peach and gray. But this was *his* room.

Slipping off the bed, she walked over to the dresser, consumed with fascination to know everything she could about him. She picked up a silver hairbrush and caressed the smooth hard metal. Just like him, aggressively masculine.

Being with Luke made her feel as if she'd never had any experience with men, despite having lived with Paul for three years. But she could see now that in those years she'd never really connected with him, not on the deepest, most intimate level. It was crazy that she'd feel closer to Luke than the man she'd lived with.

Why did she feel this? What did she know about him? She knew his strength, his sense of humor, the way they laughed at the same things. He was a very intense man and would probably be difficult to live with, she could see that. But he was also very tender. He wasn't afraid to show his vulnerability. He was strong and tough, but he could actually admit to something as human as jealousy.

And then there was that instinctive sense that she was utterly safe with him. Why was that? How could she trust him so implicitly? He was a man of mystery. Maybe it was because, in some ways, he reminded her of her father. She shook her head with a sudden feeling of embarrassment. Was she falling into some kind of classic Freudian pattern?

And yet, of course, in other ways he was a complete stranger.

Was he a happy man? She'd sensed something bleak in him. Was that part of him, or was he nursing a recent disappointment? He said he was a workaholic, but even workaholics had a social life. Did he have close friends, was he close to his family?

Her fingers traced over the initials engraved on the back of the silver brush. *J.W.* The brush was definitely old, a lovingly cared-for heirloom. So whose initials were they—a grandfather's, an uncle's perhaps?

She wanted to know him, everything about him. On a voyage of discovery, she pulled open the top drawer of the dresser. She trailed her hand across the neat pile of white cotton underwear on one side. On the other lay a stack of neatly folded white shirts, fresh from the laundry. Running her index finger down the side of the pile she noticed something dark tucked underneath.

Moving the pile aside, her heart gave a jolt and her breath escaped in a little gasp. Beneath the shirts lay a small, dangerous-looking gun in a black holster. For a long moment she just stared stupidly at it. What was he doing with this? Slowly she reached out and picked it up. It felt heavy, substantial... and deadly. Who was this man?

"Claire," Luke said quietly behind her. There was no mistaking the note of authority.

There had to be a good explanation for this, she told herself. As if in the middle of a horrible dream, she slowly turned to look into the face of a stranger. Luke stood behind her, with only a towel wrapped around his sleek, powerful body. Cold misery crept through her.

"You have a gun." Her voice sounded husky, but much calmer than she felt.

Once again the question went numbly around her brain. Who was he? He wasn't the jewel thief...

Her mouth went dry as it suddenly hit her—Luke fit the general description of the courier, just like Herb Whittaker and Klaus Voorhees. She began to shake. "Yes, I have a gun." His expression bland, he reached out and took it gently out of her hand.

Deftly wrapping the holster around it, he tucked the weapon back in its hiding place beneath the pile of shirts.

When he turned to face her she could only stare at him, in mounting pain and horror. His hair wet from the shower, his naked chest still beaded with water, he looked calm and unruffled. His expression betrayed nothing, except for the tightness of his hard mouth.

"Claire..." He reached for her and she took an instinctive step back. "I can explain why I have a gun."

"I'm sure you can." She gave a derisive laugh. Boy, she sure knew how to pick 'em. "But you don't owe me an explanation."

What was he going to do, tell her the truth? Hardly. She was starting to feel sick inside as a horrifying wave of devastation swept over her. She backed farther away from him and he lifted one eyebrow and gave her a sardonic look.

"I think I do."

"Okay, go ahead and explain." She turned away, not wanting to watch him lie.

"When I said I was a banker, I was being a trifle misleading..."

"Only a trifle?" She turned back to him resentfully.

"What I should have said was that I handle personal investments," he continued, after giving her an impatient look. "I can get away with fewer explanations when I say banker. Besides, it guards my clients' privacy."

"That still doesn't explain why you've got a gun."

"I'm carrying a small fortune in securities to hand over to a client here. I ... have to be prepared for anything." His mouth curved in a rueful smile. "I did tell you my job involved a lot of traveling."

As lies went, it was pretty inventive and plausible. On the other hand, he could actually be telling the truth. After all, there had to be a hundred reasons why he'd have a gun, none of them having anything to do with the dreadful conclusion she'd immediately leapt to.

She began to breathe a little easier. She was forgetting one thing. They had shared something very special and he felt that way too, she was sure of it. He wouldn't lie to her.

"But if you have to carry a gun..." She had barely let herself enjoy the relief when another devastating prospect sent tendrils of fear curling around her heart. "You never told me how dangerous your job was. You could get hurt."

He smiled, that slightly mocking, wicked smile that sent her heart racing. "Don't worry about me, I can take care of myself."

"I know, I've seen that you can, but that still doesn't stop me from worrying."

Luke's expression sobered and something like remorse seemed to cloud his eyes. "Come here." His voice was husky as he pulled her into his arms and held her close.

Nestled against his hard body, she laid her cheek against his shoulder and inhaled the clean scent of his skin, wondering if she could drown in this pleasure.

"Claire..." There was indecision in his pause, and she could feel his tension through the arms that held her so close. Then he gave a small, tired sigh.

"What is it, Luke?" She raised her head to look at him, into his troubled eyes.

But the next moment they had cleared and he smiled, a slow, intimate smile. He planted a kiss on the tip of her nose. "Why don't you go get changed? I'll give you an hour, then I'll come by to get you," he finished in a husky, suggestive drawl that made her want to nix that plan and crawl back into bed.

Instead, she got dressed and went back to her room. The phone was ringing as she let herself in her own door.

"I guess you must have realized that I didn't have a chance to search Voorhees's room this afternoon," her father said without preamble.

"No, really?" Her heart sank at his words and she knew what was coming, but she asked anyway. "Now what?"

"We'll have to do it again, this evening."

She knew it! "It'll have to be later this evening." Nothing was going to stop her from meeting Luke.

"Why?"

"Because I have a date for dinner."

"Dalton again, I suppose." He sounded disgruntled and impatient.

"Yes, and you're wrong about him you know." She explained all about the intruder the night before.

James snorted. "That doesn't mean anything. I'm sure he's our man and he works with an accomplice, a young lady by the name of Nikki Jones."

"Nikki Jones! Tiny little Nikki, couldn't you have picked someone a little more plausible?"

He sighed. "When are you going to realize that looks can be deceiving?"

Odd, Luke had said exactly those same words. No, she wouldn't get back on that merry-go-round of suspicion again.

Her father continued. "I'll be watching you after dinner. As soon as I see you make contact with Voorhees I'll go and do my thing." Her father's voice brought her back from the spinning chaos of her thoughts. "Something that might be helpful—he usually goes to the casino after dinner."

Without another word he hung up and Claire put down the phone. She headed for the shower, trying to shrug off the disturbing seeds of doubt that her father had once again stirred up with his insistence that Luke was the thief. Even though she believed in Luke, she couldn't help feeling uneasy.

And Klaus Voorhees again! She shuddered. The man gave her the creeps. She dreaded the prospect of spending any more time with that sleazeball. It would be a long, uncomfortable evening fending him off.

Stepping out of the shower stall, she quickly toweled herself dry. How was she going to slip away from Luke? She stewed over the problem as she slipped into the short black dress she'd worn the first night. There was only one thing to do. The old "phone call from work" ploy. She couldn't think up anything more creative and she was so tired of lying.

Picking up the phone, she dialed James's number, praying he hadn't already left.

A smile curved her lips at the sound of the familiar Scottish brogue. He'd landed her in a huge mess, but she loved him and there wasn't anything she wouldn't do for him. After he agreed to call her at ten, she hung up and finished getting ready, amazed at how sharp her mind had suddenly become.

She knew exactly how she could pull this off. As long as she didn't dwell on the possibility of Luke being a thief, everything would be fine. Anyway, as far as she was concerned, he was still innocent until proven guilty.

Somehow, once she'd come to that way of looking at things, she felt suddenly more in control. Just as she applied the last touch of lipstick to her mouth she heard a knock and her heart began to pound.

She opened the door to see Luke in his tuxedo, looking so breathtakingly handsome that her heart skipped a beat. He stood smiling down at her, and let his gaze roam over her slowly and deliberately, with hungry appreciation that sent a wave of heat right down to her toes.

"I like that dress on you. It brings back warm memories." Now that teasing glint in his eye no longer made her feel defensive. "You know, you never did explain what you were doing on my balcony." Sly mockery tugged at one corner of his mouth.

"No, and I'm not going to. Your ego is healthy enough."

He just laughed at her arched look and Claire was thankful he didn't pursue the subject any further. She hated lying to him, but she'd have to do it again at ten o'clock, so she'd better harden herself.

The dining room looked as it had that first night—was it only the day before yesterday? The muted glitter of silver and crystal, the richly dressed women and their escorts in tuxedos or white dinner jackets.

There was no sign of James, but she did see Nikki sitting with a man at another table. And this was supposed to be Luke's accomplice in crime? Claire had to smile to herself. The only person on this island that she could easily believe to be a criminal was Klaus Voorhees.

But she didn't allow any of her worries to intrude during dinner, just enjoyed Luke's fascinated, seductive attention.

"Excuse me, Miss Sterling? You have a phone call."

She gave a start at the waiter's discreetly delivered message. Was it ten o'clock already? Her heart began to pound. She'd almost forgotten the task that lay ahead.

Reluctantly she stood. Luke stood, too, and looked down at her inquiringly. The last thing she wanted to do was spend the evening with Voorhees. She'd rather be safely with Luke.

"I've been expecting this call, it's the Pfeiffer estate again. We weren't able to conclude the business this afternoon." It was almost impossible to look at him while she lied. "I'm afraid this might take a while."

Her fingers dug into the back of the tapestry-covered chair as she teetered on the edge of anxiety.

"Can we meet later?"

She sighed, relieved by his acceptance of her explanation, but feeling guilty that he trusted her so implicitly.

"I'd like that very much." When this was all over she wouldn't leave without telling him the truth. "Where shall I meet you?"

"How about in my room?" He glanced at his watch. "About midnight?"

"That sounds fine."

"Good." The smile in his eyes held a promise that made her knees weak. "I'm not letting you out of my sight longer than that. Don't be late."

"I won't," she promised, and quickly turned and left. The sooner she got this thing done, the sooner they'd be together.

Heading quickly for the casino, she kept a sharp eye out for James. He promised he'd be watching her, but where was he concealing himself? And he'd better be right about Voorhees's habits, she didn't want to spend half her time looking for him.

But as she entered the casino she spotted him right away, standing by the roulette table. Even if he was a creep, she had to admit he cut a pretty impressive figure. Tall, dark, and snakily handsome, he looked very sharp in black tie, fitting right in with the other movers and shakers who crowded the room, playing for high stakes.

Even from a distance, she had no problem believing *him* to be the ruthless criminal James suspected.

Taking a deep breath to steady her suddenly failing nerves, she made herself approach him. Gritting her teeth, she plunged in at the deep end. "Hello, there, remember me?"

He turned and looked at her, and she could tell that for a moment he hadn't the faintest idea who she was. Every woman probably looked the same to him. His dark gaze ran over her, stripping off her clothes in a way that made her feel demeaned.

"Oh, yes, the lady from the pool. You ran away before we got a chance to get to know each other."

"Yes, and that's why I came back tonight."

He smiled with such conceit and arrogance she had to bite back the urge to knee him in the groin. This was going to be the longest two hours of her life.

"Do you dance?" she asked artlessly.

"A little." His eyes were still on her body, on her legs revealed by the short dress.

"Would you care to go to the Hibiscus Room? They have a very good band there tonight."

"I'd rather go up to *my* room, where we can be alone."

Did the guy only have one line? she wondered in disgust. "Yes, I've been thinking about that," she murmured uncertainly. "I—I think I'd like that, too, but..." Biting her lower lip, she glanced up at him through her lashes, trying her best to imitate Marilyn Monroe at her most innocently provocative. "I need to...to get to know you a little better. And besides, maybe a little wine might help build my nerve. I—I've never done this sort of thing before."

"Then by all means...let's go and find some."

He put an arm around her shoulder to escort her out of the room and five seconds later that hand had found its way to her hips. Her stomach churned as he blatantly squeezed her bottom. She felt like applying an elbow to his ribs, but gritted her teeth and checked her watch. An hour and forty-five minutes left. This was carrying duty way too far.

The bar was crowded and noisy, the air stale with cigarette smoke, but at least there were people around.

At least here he'd have to limit himself to surreptitious groping. God knows, she wouldn't put anything past this snake, including rape. Whatever happened, she mustn't allow him to get her anywhere alone.

Taking a corner table, Voorhees ordered a bottle of wine and poured her a glass with a lazy conceit that made her want to grab the ice bucket off the bar and dump it in his lap.

His kind were all too easy to read—he had no respect for her, no appreciation of her as anything but a tool for his satisfaction. His manner, his voice, everything about him proclaimed that he was a swaggering bully. She took a small sip of the wine, and fervently hoped he got into a heap of trouble from his boss when James took the coronet away from him.

Instinct made her absolutely certain now that this man was the courier. And then with a spurt of shock she thought of another possibility. Maybe he'd been whiling away his time picking up a bonus. After all, the man was strong and athletic, he'd made sure everyone noticed that on the diving platform.

Why hadn't it occurred to her before? Klaus Voorhees could be both the courier *and* the hotel thief!

He leaned toward her, trying to press his leg between her knees. Claire choked down another sip of wine. Sickening as it was, she could put up with his pawing, knowing that he was heading for his just deserts.

She disengaged her legs and gave him a brilliant smile. "Would you like to dance?"

As they joined the other couples swaying to the slow reggae beat, she consoled herself with the thought that at least he couldn't do much on the dance floor.

It was no surprise when he pressed much too intimately against her, but she noticed thankfully that, though he was obviously gripped by sexual excitement, she couldn't feel any evidence of physical arousal. Maybe that was his problem. Maybe bullying women was the only way he could feel like a real man.

"May I cut in?"

She turned her head to see Herb Whittaker's smiling face.

Voorhees barely glanced at him. "No, you can't. Beat it." He swung Claire roughly away.

A frown creased Herb's good-natured face and he pugnaciously stood his ground. "Are you all right, Claire?"

"I said, beat it." Now Voorhees lifted his head to glare at the other man with intimidating viciousness.

"Is this man bullying you?" Herb ignored him to look earnestly at her.

"No, no, he's not. I'm fine," she hurried to reassure her would-be rescuer. She wouldn't put it past this Neanderthal to slug him and she didn't want poor Herb to get hurt.

"Are you sure?" He still looked worried.

"She's very sure." Voorhees had stopped all pretense of dancing, his body tensed as if a hairbreadth from exploding. He fixed Herb with a corrosive sneer. "Now get lost, pal."

But Herb's gaze remained steadfastly on her. Underneath that sweet, gentle exterior was a chivalrous and very brave man.

"Claire, is this man bothering you?"

"I'm fine Herb, really." Claire smiled, trying to sound carefree and unaware of the latent threat of violence that emanated from Voorhees like a poisonous cloud.

Whittaker looked at her closely, then finally shrugged and walked away. Claire yearned to run after him and explain why she was sticking with this low-life jerk. Herb seemed like such a decent man, she hated to imagine what he must be thinking of her.

The music stopped and she snatched at the opportunity to get away, even for a few moments. She extricated herself from Voorhees's grip and began to move away. "Will you excuse me? I'll be right back."

He grabbed her arm roughly. "Where are you going?"

A sick shiver of fear trembled down her spine. This man was definitely dangerous. "Just to the ladies' room."

"Okay," he grunted reluctantly.

As she hurried thankfully away she saw him saunter back to the table and pour himself another glass of wine. He wouldn't leave now. He'd spent money on her and he expected the payoff.

The corridor to the ladies' room led past a dense bank of potted palms. As she went by, a hand reached out and grabbed her, pulling her in behind the foliage as she yelped in surprise.

She looked up and felt the blood drain from her cheeks. "Luke!" She gave a disbelieving gasp. "What are you doing here?"

"Come with me." His voice was as granite hard as his expression and his grip tightened as she tried to pull away.

"But I have to go back," she said desperately.

"No. It's over, Claire. It's all over." The gritty finality in his words made her go cold inside.

His face was icy pale except for a hectic slash of color along his cheekbones, his mouth compressed in a hard, cruel line.

"But you don't understand." Trying to loosen her wrist from his iron grip, she stumbled to keep up with his long stride as he marched her down the corridor, away from the bar.

"Yes, I do. I understand more than you think," he said tightly as he pulled her along with him.

"Luke, please!" She tried to pull out of his grip but it only tightened.

Oh, God, she'd give anything to be able to explain to him what she was doing with that man. All of this could have been so simple if she'd been able to explain from the beginning. It wasn't that she couldn't trust Luke, but it was her father's secret, not hers to tell.

And right now she didn't think he'd listen to any explanations. There was something so coldly grim and forbidding about him, like a stranger. Fate was not on her side. Three times she'd snuck away from him to do her father's bidding, and all three times he'd found her, showing her up in the worst possible light. She must look like some kind of nymphomaniac.

"Luke, we have to talk," she pleaded desperately. Somehow she'd have to get James to explain.

"We will, in a minute." He bit off the terse reply. And then she realized he was taking her outside, not upstairs to the room.

Taking a softly lit path through the shrubbery, they came to one of the small, stone guest cottages. Luke knocked softly.

"Where are we?" she demanded. "Whose room is this?"

Luke didn't say anything and for the first time she began to feel afraid. What was going on here? The door opened and Luke stepped inside, pulling her in behind him, not roughly but with a leashed anger. She blinked against the unaccustomed light, then gasped in shock to see Nikki closing the door behind them.

"And now we're all here. One big happy family." The other woman gave her a grimly sarcastic smile.

But she got an even bigger shock when she turned to see James standing by the patio doors, hands in pockets, looking out onto the moonswept beach.

"Dad!" She dimly realized that Luke wasn't holding her wrist anymore. Confused and frightened, she rushed over to her father and put her arms around him, looking him over anxiously. "Are you all right? What's happening?"

Gently but firmly, he put her away from him. "I'm fine, girl, now don't fuss."

His stern tone of voice and the warning look in his black, glittering eyes told her to get a grip. She took a deep breath and felt her panic diminish a little.

"I'll tell you what's happening."

It took her a second to recognize the voice behind her as Luke's. So cold, so forbidding. The voice of a stranger. Was this the voice of the man she'd held trembling in her arms only a few hours ago?

She turned to see a face as hard and cold as his voice. The face of a stranger.

"The game is up. I know what you're doing here."

"What are you talking about?" A cold chill spread through her veins. James was right about Luke after all.

"I just want to know how you knew about the coronet." Luke ignored her question as his hard, glittering eyes focused on James. Then they slid over to her and she flinched to see the coldness there, like pale chips of ice. "That was your job—wasn't it?—keeping Voorhees busy while your father went to work." His hard mouth twisted with derision. "God, I've been so dense. All this time I thought you were after anything you could pick up, but it wasn't till this afternoon that I realized you even knew about the coronet."

"Leave my daughter out of this." Her father said threateningly as he put an arm around her and pulled her protectively against his side. "She came here for one reason only—to stop me."

She stared at Luke in shock, not knowing what to say, what to do. Inside she felt terribly numb, but she should be thankful. When it wore off, the pain was going to be unbearable.

"Well, she failed miserably. But I won't." Again that hard, cold voice penetrated her deadened senses.

"Who are you?" James asked slowly.

She felt a flutter of pride that even in this dire situation her father had lost nothing of his air of command, even facing a man as formidable as Luke was right now.

"I'll ask the questions here," Luke stated.

"But if you want any answers, son, you'd better be a little more forthcoming." James's tone was mild and unconcerned, and Claire could see that Luke was slightly taken aback.

Then James moved past her toward Luke, his hands in the pockets of his dinner jacket, looking impossibly relaxed and urbane. Claire could only stare, she'd never seen her father in this sort of situation before and could only marvel at his calm control when he had to know he was up the creek without a paddle.

"I think we'd all better explain ourselves, don't you?" he said to Luke. "And I have a feeling I'll have to go first." A wry smile curved his lips as he sank down onto the couch, looking as at-home as a man entertaining guests. "Because otherwise I'll never find out what you're doing here." He paused and fixed Luke with a shrewd stare. "Am I going to find out?"

"Possibly." Luke's answer was very quiet as he watched James's movements, never once taking his hard, glittering eyes off the older man.

Unperturbed, James nodded in resignation. "Just as I thought."

None of this made any sense. What the hell were they talking about?

"Shall we all sit down, then?" Unruffled, James waved a hand around the sitting area in invitation.

Nikki scooted quickly over and plonked herself down on the couch beside James, and Claire suddenly remembered again that she was there. This whole thing was too unreal. Luke took one of the armchairs, his gaze never straying from James.

Her father turned to her in bland inquiry. "Are you going to join us, Claire?"

She couldn't believe he was being so casual, but she tried to take her cue from him as to how to behave. Or *try* to behave. But she wouldn't let James stand alone, no matter how overwhelmed this situation made her feel.

As she sank down into the other armchair, James slowly looked around at them. "I suppose I'd better start at the beginning."

"Yes, that would be a good place to start." Luke wasn't nearly as relaxed as her father. His voice still vibrated with tension and anger.

Yet once again she was struck by the similarity between the two men, that air of leashed forcefulness. In

James the years had mellowed a power that was still formidable, while Luke radiated a keen intensity as invincible as a force of nature.

"Before I start, I just want to get one thing clear," James began. "You're not the one pulling these other jobs, are you?" It was a statement, not a question.

Luke slowly shook his head. "No, I'm not."

"That's what I was afraid of." James gave a grim smile.

Claire stared at them both in confusion. Why was her father afraid? And if Luke wasn't the other jewel thief, how did he know about the coronet?

Her mouth went dry with fear as all the pieces fell sickeningly into place. He'd been the one they were looking for all this time. Luke *was* the courier, after all.

11

"So..." THE GRIM LOOK hardened on her father's face as he regarded Luke. "If you're not the jewel thief, or the courier, then... who are you?"

"My name, as you know, is Luke Dalton." He seemed to look straight through her, his face, his voice, everything about him became even more hard and dispassionate. "I work for the British government."

James sighed and nodded his head with a small, wry smile. "I see. Well, my story begins with Prince Ottolon of Wittgenstein, who also happens to be my old friend Karl." James went on to outline the events that had led to his pursuit of the coronet, and his conviction that his unique abilities could succeed where the police were powerless.

As her father spoke, Claire watched Luke, she couldn't help herself. He stared intently at James right now, his face hard and implacable, almost frightening.

She rubbed her upper arms, suddenly cold despite the sultry air. Had it only been three days since she'd arrived here? It felt like a lifetime. Had it only been three days ago that she stood at that reception desk, feeling Luke's attention focused on her, just as surely as she now felt he had locked her out?

The magic was over and her fantasy in paradise had turned into a cold, bleak Monday morning, like she knew all along it would. What she hadn't known was how much it would hurt.

"And so I came here to find the courier and get the thing back for Karl." James had finally come to the end of his story and looked at the other man expectantly.

She became aware of the quiet—the soft sounds of the tropical night, the crickets chirping, the rush of the surf outside the open sliding-glass doors.

Inside it was a strange tableau. Nikki sat chewing thoughtfully on her lip, her eyes focused on her running shoes. James was watching Luke dispassionately, while Luke still pinned James with an impenetrable look.

With a feeling of despair, Claire knew she couldn't even hope to guess at what was going on behind the implacable mask of his face.

"Why did you have to bring your daughter into this?"

She gave a gasp of surprise and felt a small lift of hope. Luke's first question concerned *her*. But that hope vanished almost immediately. He didn't even glance at her, as if she wasn't even there.

"Bring her into this!" James exploded.

At almost the same moment she said indignantly, "He didn't bring me into this. I came of my own free will."

"She has a disgusting excess of free will," her father snorted. "Would you believe she threatened to turn me in to the police? *Me*, her own father! Would you believe it?"

For the first time Luke's grim mouth curved and widened into a smile of genuine amusement. "Yes, I can believe it," he murmured softly.

His bright eyes turned toward her, with a gleam in their depths that told her *I know you*, and had her heart pounding even harder in her chest.

"I came here to stop my father from getting himself hurt, or arrested. When I realized he wasn't going to be dissuaded, I had to help him, what other choice did I have?"

Inside she felt miserable. What did it matter whether she explained herself to Luke or not? Did it matter what he thought of her? Whatever had happened between them was over and done with. It was finished.

He held her gaze for a long moment, then looked away with a sigh and mumbled under his breath something that sounded like, "Thank God for that."

"From the very beginning I felt I was being watched, was that you?" Her father's tone was almost conversational, how could he be so calm?

"Sometimes me, sometimes Nikki." Luke nodded to his partner.

"But if you didn't know until today that we were after the coronet, why were you watching me from the start?"

"You're James Sterling. You had a very successful career, and were never caught. I just assumed you were bored with the straight and narrow and were looking for some action, this time with your daughter as your apprentice."

With icy-cold clarity, understanding dawned. So, right from the beginning he'd thought she was a thief, too. That explained the intense attention, the lifted passport.

Once again he looked at James. "I've been tailing your daughter ever since she got here."

And she'd sensed it from the very beginning. This would teach her to trust her instincts. No, she would not cry, she would not show her pain.

"So you spent a whole day entertaining me." Her voice sounded surprisingly steady. "I'm sorry you went to so much trouble for my sake. What a dreadful waste of your time."

Luke turned to look at her. A dull, red flush grazed his cheekbones, but his blue eyes were hard and guarded. "It wasn't simply for your sake. We had to keep that yacht under surveillance and you gave me a good reason for being there. While we were swimming, Samuel kept watch..."

"And later you took over from the hill," she finished, wondering dully at the pure, gut-wrenching pain tearing her apart right now. She let out a shaky, sarcastic laugh. "How could I have been so stupid? It never dawned on me, what you were doing. Well, I feel much better now. At least your day wasn't a complete waste of time."

"What do you expect?" he retorted, then struggled to regain his composure. "I thought you were a thief."

Once again he turned toward James. He didn't even want to look at her. "Having a jewel thief around complicated our plans. We couldn't afford to have the coronet stolen from the courier. It wasn't till this afternoon that I realized you were after it."

"What tipped you off?" James asked calmly.

"When you had your daughter occupy Klaus at the pool, I put two and two together. Whittaker looks very much like Voorhees."

James gave a grim, dry smile. "I see. Very clever."

Her head was whirling. So when he showed up both times he *had* been tailing her. All that talk about jealousy was just an act. While she . . . she'd made a big fat fool of herself.

"And this evening I had further proof you must be here specifically for the coronet because, thanks to Nikki and the local police, we caught the person who stole your friend Maisie's jewels." Once again Luke flicked a glance over at her, but it was quick and dispassionate. He didn't *want* to really look at her, Claire realized miserably.

"And who might that be?" James inquired.

"A little guy named Howie Crump."

Claire gasped in shock. "Not that little pest!"

Luke turned to look at her and she saw a grim shadow of amusement in his eyes as they held hers.

"The drunken loser bit was a pretty good cover." Nikki spoke up for the first time. "And it gave him a chance to get up close and check out the merchandise."

And then Claire remembered how he'd hung off her neck, only inches away from her diamond pendant, and he'd done the same thing to the redhead in the bar.

"It's Voorhees, isn't it?" James said sharply. "He *is* the courier. He's got the coronet."

Luke said nothing for a few moments, then nodded reluctantly. "Yes."

James sat up and leaned toward him, the negligent air discarded. "You have to let me get it back."

"I can't, not yet."

"Then that brings us to the last question. What's your part in all this?"

Claire strained forward, clutching the arms of the chair until the strands of wicker dug deeply into her palms.

All this time sitting watching him, listening to him talk, she felt as if he were going farther and farther away from her. He truly was a stranger, this man with whom she'd been as intimate as two people could be.

Luke turned to James again. "Does the name Enrico Espinoza mean anything to you?"

Her father shook his head. "I can't say it does."

"He's the man who commissioned the theft of your coronet."

"And your interest in him?"

"Drug dealing, arms smuggling, murder...you name it." His voice took on a harsh edge. "Nikki, here, is with the Drug Enforcement Agency. We're part of a joint deal to capture Espinoza. We've been after him for a long time and this is the closest we've ever got. He's on a private island somewhere around here—we don't know where, there are so many islands in these seas. Our only chance to find him is the courier."

"But how will you manage it?" James asked.

"We have to wait for him to be picked up."

"And then?"

"Somehow I'll trade places with him before that happens."

Cold fear tightened around her heart. How was Luke going to do that? Did he mean he'd have to kill Voorhees, arrest him?

Her head was still reeling from trying to assimilate what Luke had said. He wasn't a criminal, at least, but his true purpose for being here was even more frightening. Drugs, terrorism, murder... his words opened up a murky world that chilled her blood.

Luke went on. "Now do you understand why we had to make sure you didn't get too close to Voorhees?"

Yes. It was all too clear now, too humiliatingly clear. Luke went on talking, but Claire felt herself going slowly numb. All that time and attention he'd lavished on her, all the fascinated pursuit—her stomach clenched painfully—even the wild, urgent lovemaking, all of it had been make-believe. She had been an assignment. Bile rose in her throat, she had to get away.

Abruptly she got to her feet and headed blindly for the door.

"LET HER GO." James spoke softly but his voice had a core of steel and Luke unwillingly sank back into his seat. "What's happened, happened. There's not much I can do about it, but I won't let you hurt her anymore." His eyes looked very black, glittering with a deadly promise.

A promise that would be kept. Luke had been up against ruthlessness before, but rarely did he see anything approaching the determination and willpower of Claire's father.

"I just want you to know that I never planned on any of this happening. You see, from the very beginning I thought..."

"You thought she was a thief." James eyed him shrewdly. "Naturally you had to keep her under surveillance, and naturally you were attracted to her."

He felt like a bastard. "She thinks I just used her, but that's not true. She probably hates me."

James's smile was grim. "All the more reason to leave her alone. Better that she hate you, than regret you. Do you understand, lad?" His voice had lost its aggressive edge, but there was no mistaking the veiled threat still hanging between them. "Now, what about the coronet?"

"Don't worry about it. When this is all over I'll deliver it to you personally."

James fixed him with a penetrating look. "You don't have to go to that much trouble, just get it to me."

"It won't be any trouble, and you know I have more than one reason to see you."

"What for? Let it go. There's no future in it." James stopped and raised a finger toward him. "Don't get me wrong, just because I accepted what's happened doesn't mean I like it. I'm warning you, if you ever hurt my girl again, I'll make life very unpleasant for you."

"I believe you will," Luke said with feeling. "But you'd better start now if you want to stop me, because I have to go and see Claire before I leave tonight. I have to let her know."

The older man lurched to his feet. "Know what?" he demanded impatiently. "You know as well as I do it'll only make things worse. Let it go, Dalton."

Iron fingers closed over Luke's arm and James glared into his face. He looked down at the restraining hand and deliberately pulled his arm from the older man's grasp.

"I suppose it's very selfish of me," Luke said quietly, "but I have to let her know that it wasn't all an act. I can't let her go on thinking that I used her. Believe me, I don't want to hurt her any more than I have. You're just going to have to trust me on this one, Sterling."

Almost for the first time since coming into the room he glanced over at Nikki sitting silently on the couch. "Is everything set to go?"

She nodded. "Samuel's on standby. We're just waiting for our man to move."

"Fine." He smiled at her. "Good luck and be careful. I wouldn't want to lose you, partner."

"No fear of that. But you'd better go get a few things off your chest so that you're thinking straight when we move." He saw the sympathy in her eyes and knew she wasn't just talking about the assignment.

No, he couldn't let himself be distracted. Many more lives than his were at stake if he wasn't working at his peak.

He turned his gaze to James, expecting another attempt to stop him. But instead James held out his hand, his expression sober. "Take care of yourself, son."

He took the proffered hand and gripped it firmly. "Don't worry, my hide is extremely precious to me. I take very good care of it. And now I have even more reason to."

James raised one dark eyebrow and said wryly, "But you're not bulletproof."

And suddenly he was aware that he wanted to know this man better, much better. Son-in-law to a criminal genius? The thought made him laugh. James began to chuckle, too, and somehow Luke knew they were laughing at the same thing.

Luke stepped out of the cottage into the dark, moist, fragrant night, filled with the restless rush of the sea, and headed along the stone pathway toward the lights of the hotel glittering above the dark palms.

No matter how badly he needed to see Claire, James was right. He couldn't tell her how he felt, not right now. He couldn't put that burden on her shoulders. Not when there was the possibility that he might not make it back.

He shrugged that dark thought aside. He didn't like dwelling on it. Too much like tempting fate.

THE QUICK, VIOLENT BOUT of tears had subsided and Claire lay on the bed feeling drained and exhausted, but conscious that life would go on. She'd jumped into this fully aware of the risks, and deliberately disregarded them. Now she had to deal with the consequences.

She understood everything. Luke's moments of reluctance, of holding himself back. *She was a job to him.* Worse than that, she was someone he despised—a thief. He'd had to act a part, and boy, was he a good actor.

What a stupid fool she'd made of herself, a complete and utter fool, actually believing that he felt as overcome, as affected, as she by what had happened between them.

She raised her head a little from the damp coverlet and wiped at the tears still clinging to her cheeks.

All she wanted to do now was go home and forget it ever happened. The sick, futile feelings of anger and embarrassment would fade with time. There was no reason to feel so devastated.

The dark bedroom was quiet, but suddenly she felt the prickling awareness that she wasn't alone. Lifting her head, she saw him standing silently in her balcony doorway.

Quickly she sat up and wiped at her wet face. In the darkness she couldn't make out his features, just the outline of his body in the diffuse light from below. But she knew him. He was imprinted on her heart and would never be erased.

"It's you." Her voice came out thick and husky.

"Yes, it's me." She heard the smile and the uncertainty in his deep voice. He was usually so sure of himself.

Reaching over to the bedside table, she clicked on the lamp. Soft light filled the space between them and reflected in those pale blue eyes. He was watching her with that glittering intensity she knew so well. In spite of what she'd heard in his voice, there was no smile on his face.

"I don't have a lot of time so I'm just going to say it. When I made love to you, it had nothing to do with duty. I wanted you, and I couldn't help myself."

She ruthlessly repressed the urge to believe him. "I understand." Her voice was soft.

"If only I could believe you did. You feel used—"

"Luke." She cut him off quickly. "It doesn't matter what I feel. It doesn't really matter what happened. You had your reasons for being here and I had mine. Somewhere in the middle we ended up having some pretty hot sex. We both knew the fantasy would come to an end, and it has. There's nothing more to say."

"There's *plenty* more to say." He spoke through gritted teeth. "But not here, and not now."

She understood what he was trying to tell her. Sometimes, in his job, he had to do things he didn't enjoy. He wasn't a cruel man. He might have fooled her about many things, but she would stake her life that he didn't enjoy hurting people.

Besides, she was a big girl. And all along she'd known the risk of playing with fire.

She lifted her chin and tried to look calm and composed. "When is this switch supposed to take place?"

The last thing she wanted was for him to see how frightened and hurt and alone she felt. He'd only blame himself, and misplaced guilt was the last thing he needed to deal with right now as he headed into God knew what kind of danger.

"Maybe tonight. I'm hoping tonight," he said quietly. "As a matter of fact, I can't stay too long."

A painful hand tightened around her heart. "Then you'd better go."

"Yes." He hesitated and looked into her eyes and she saw pure, unadulterated pain. "Claire, it wasn't *all* an act. I wanted you. In spite of everything I believed you to be, I wanted you. I'm sorry I hurt you."

She had to ruthlessly hold back the tears that sprang into her eyes. Suddenly it was all so painfully clear.

Somewhere along the way, somehow, she'd fallen in love with Luke Dalton. In spite of not knowing anything about him, in spite of everything.

"It's all right. I understand." She'd be damned if she let him walk away from here, into unknown dangers, thinking he'd broken her heart.

She slipped off the bed and walked over to him. Stopping a few inches away she looked up into his face, his pale eyes grave and still as he looked down into hers.

"Goodbye, Luke. Take care of yourself. And thank you for a wonderful interlude." The smile trembled on her lips, but she forced herself to hold his gaze as she leaned up and placed her mouth against his.

His kiss was soft and gentle and brief, then he leaned away from her with that gravity still darkening his eyes. "I'll be back. I promised your father I'd bring him the coronet. What are your plans?"

"Back to work, of course." She gave a small laugh. Laughing was the last thing she felt like doing. "I have a boss who's extremely understanding, but even he has his limits."

He nodded gravely. "I'll come and see you."

"That'll be lovely." She had a lump in her throat that made it difficult to talk, but she was proud of herself for managing to sound so natural.

His eyes became dark and disturbed. "Claire..." He stopped and let out his breath in a sharp sigh of frustration.

Whatever he'd been about to say, probably more apologies, he'd changed his mind. It was all right. She already knew how badly he felt.

Moving to the door, he opened it, then turned and looked at her. "I'll be back," he said again before going out and shutting the door quietly behind him.

Hot tears oozed slowly down her cheeks in big, slow drops. He was gone. Despite his promise, she'd probably never see him again. Even if she did, what did she imagine was going to happen? That he'd declare his undying love for her... Hardly!

No, only fools like her did things like that. But how could she be in love with a man she'd known so briefly? This was real life, not a fairy tale. But she'd been living in a fairy tale and at some point she had started believing it. She had no one to blame but herself if she hurt. Because, fairy tale or not, there was nothing imaginary about the pain knifing through her.

But how was she going to stop her body from wanting him? And how was she going to stop her heart from loving him? She couldn't imagine feeling this way for any other man, ever. For the first time, the future looked dull and empty. For the first time, nothing, not even her job, offered any compensation.

There was a time—was that only last night?—when she thought the fantasy would be enough. But now she knew it would never be enough. She'd never be able to find comfort in memories. They would only be a cruel reminder of her loss.

12

CLAIRE STOOD on the stone terrace of her father's château, looking down with unseeing eyes into the gray mist that veiled the Mediterranean a thousand meters below. It looked like they were in for a major storm, but it hardly mattered to her. She was dangerously close to despair.

Through the cool, moisture-laden air came the distant snarl of a sports car challenging the twists and turns of the Grand Corniche as the mountainside highway wound along the Riviera.

Could it only be the third day since they'd left Bateaux? Barely a week since he'd come into her life and irrevocably changed her world? And still no word.

But what did she expect, a day-by-day report? She rubbed her sweater-clad arms against the winter chill, impatient with herself. Why had she come home with her father, anyway? She should have gone back to Toronto, back to work. Even if Luke did return the coronet to James in person, what was she expecting from him? What could they have to talk about? Nothing. They'd only known each other for three days.

The noise of the car was getting louder. She could see it now, and idly watched the small blue dot zigzagging its way around the hairpin turns that led up the mountain to the village.

One more day and she was definitely going home. She couldn't spend the rest of her life moping around, waiting for things to happen. And there again, what was she expecting to happen? That Luke would fall to his knees, declare his undying love, ask her to marry him and they'd live happily ever after?

This wasn't a movie or a fairy tale, this was real life and it was time for her to check back into it. It was bad enough that she'd fallen in love with a complete stranger, but did she have to make matters worse by nurturing expectations that could only lead to pain and disappointment?

The little blue car had reached the stone walls and massive iron gates of the tiny village, gates that, since the year 1134, still closed every night at midnight.

When she had come here to stay as a young girl that nightly ritual had made her feel secure and peaceful, safe and snug in her father's little mountaintop haven. It would be a long time before she felt that kind of peace again. It would be a long time before she got over Luke.

The little blue car had disappeared from sight as it passed through the open gates, then came into view again as it nosed slowly along the narrow street. Not very many tourists left behind the glamour of Cannes to head up the mountain to the ancient village, fewer still made the trip in winter.

The car turned into the cobbled courtyard beside the château and her heart suddenly began to pound. Was it possible?

Unable to look, she jerked her gaze away again toward the hazy panorama of the sea, trying to concentrate on the dark mass of heavy cloud billowing on the horizon. A car door slammed and she whirled back, too late. Whoever it was had already gone around to the front entrance.

Rushing through the French doors into the living room, she stopped dead, her heart pounding in her chest like a runaway train. The bang of the brass knocker reverberated through the quiet house. Then she heard Albert's slow, deliberate tread ringing on the terrazzo. She glimpsed his short, balding figure as he walked in stately slowness toward the front door.

Calm down. Compose yourself. Wait to see how he behaves. If he wanted her, he'd show it. If he didn't, then there was no reason for him to know how she felt. Every nerve straining, she forced herself to go back out on the terrace.

But a few seconds later she couldn't stand the suspense anymore and walked back into the living room just as Albert opened the hall door wider. His piercing blue eyes looked questioningly at her through small, wire-framed glasses before he stepped aside and ushered in the visitor with Old World formality.

Holding her breath, Claire stared at the open doorway and felt her heart stop beating. When Nikki came striding into the room, it lurched with a sharp jolt of disappointment.

The small blonde stopped short, clearly surprised to see her there. "Oh... hello." She looked uncomfortable and her gaze darted around the room. "I was expecting to see James."

"He'll be here soon." Claire forced a smile. "Won't you sit down?"

Nikki sank into one of the tapestry armchairs with a tense and guarded air, but Claire barely noticed. Swamped by the bitter sense of let-down, as painful as a physical blow, she tried to tell herself that she'd known all along he wouldn't come.

"Shall I bring in some refreshments for the young lady?" Albert suggested.

Belatedly, she remembered her duty as a hostess and tried not to think about Luke. "Oh, yes... Can I offer you something to eat... drink?"

"I wouldn't say no to a cup of coffee."

Nikki smiled, but she looked tired and drawn, and there was a gravity behind her eyes Claire had never seen before.

She turned to Albert, standing patiently erect by the door, and found him shrewdly sizing up Nikki Jones through his thick lenses. The old dear was a good judge of character. In this case, he'd clearly concluded Nikki was another of James's typical foibles—a pretty woman who was far too young for him.

"Coffee, please, Albert."

With a formal nod, he turned to leave. Never once had she seen Albert hurry or lose that imperturbable calm. He passed James on the way out and shot him a judgmental look that made his employer scowl impatiently back at him.

Claire had to smile to herself. Those two were always sniping, but they couldn't live without each other. Not that she could ever say that to Albert, he'd be shocked, he didn't like having his dignity mocked.

As James came into the room Nikki rose with relief and moved quickly toward him.

"Nikki, my dear, it's so good to see you." He moved to take her hand, a smile creasing his handsome face.

Nikki's smile of response was strained and tight. "I just came to bring you this." She reached into her canvas tote and pulled out a cloth bag, handing it over to him.

Reaching in, he took out an object swathed in blue velvet. Swiftly he removed the wrappings and held it up—the glorious coronet of Wittgenstein.

He examined it closely, his dark eyes gleaming with excitement as the jewels glowed and sparkled even in the gray light that filtered into the room. Claire felt her breath catch in awe as she, too, gazed at it.

After a few moments James wrapped it up again and put it back into its protective cloth bag.

"Thank you for bringing this back. Karl will be very happy to see it again." He put the bag on the carved antique coffee table. "How did it go? And, Luke, how is he?"

Claire held her breath and waited for Nikki's next words, but they didn't come. She looked at her and was surprised to see her expression darken.

"Well, Espinoza is dead, and Luke..." Nikki began, then stopped and looked at Claire, her eyes filling with pain and compassion.

Something had happened. Her heart became an icy stone in her chest.

She heard the distant echo of Nikki's voice. "I'm sorry to have to tell you this, but I haven't seen him since shortly after we landed at Espinoza's compound. I've filed a report that he's missing, presumed dead."

Claire heard somebody say, "No." It might even have been her. Numbly she became aware of James taking her hand.

"They're still searching for him though?" her father asked urgently.

"We won't give up till we find the...find him," Nikki finished in a quiet, tense voice.

Everything went dead and silent. Claire could see the worry on her father's face as he went on asking questions, see his eyes darting over to her, but she couldn't hear a word.

Six days. Only six days since he'd entered her life and turned it upside down, and now, in a matter of moments, he was gone. And he'd taken a part of her with him.

It had seemed ludicrous, falling in love with a man she'd just met. She'd asked herself over and over again how deep could such feelings go? She had her answer now, in the wrenching pain tearing her apart.

Albert had come in with the coffee and put it down on the table. Someone put a cup in her hand and she drank it, unaware if it was black or white, sugared or not.

Dimly she realized that Nikki was now telling James she had to leave for London to file a report, then return to Miami. But she'd promised Luke that she'd return the coronet.

"But you can't leave now," James protested. "Not in this storm."

Turning to the tall windows, Claire saw that it had become black as night outside, though it was only the middle of the afternoon. A gray curtain of heavy rain was splashing off the stone urns and glazing the terracotta. And she hadn't even noticed it begin.

"But I have to," Nikki insisted. "I have to be in London tonight."

"I hope you can get through. We get mudslides around here. We've had quite a few already this winter and the mountain roads are treacherous, they may even be washed out already. We'll find out from Albert, he knows everything around here."

"Can I at least use your phone?"

"Certainly. I'll show you where it is." He turned to Claire, his brow furrowed, his eyes probing and concerned. "Are you all right, darling?"

"Yes." She met his worried look with a small, automatic smile. She didn't feel a thing. Not a thing.

James took Nikki out of the room and Claire turned toward the open French doors and walked outside. She began shivering violently and suddenly realized that she was drenched, the rain beating on her head and plastering it to her skull, the clammy wool sweater damp against her skin.

What in God's name was she doing out here, trying to catch her death of pneumonia? She went back in again just as Nikki and James returned to the room.

Her father frowned as his gaze ran over her wet face and his dark eyes glittered with concern. "The phones are down." What else was new? They went down every time it rained. "And Nikki's going to be our guest for the night. Maybe you'd like to show her to her room and get her sorted out. Then get yourself dried off."

"Come with me." She smiled at the other woman. She must be smiling, because she could feel the muscles in her face stretching automatically. "You're just in time for lunch, too. Are you hungry?"

"Starved. I haven't had much time for meals in the past couple of days."

Taking her upstairs, she led Nikki to the room next to hers and opened the door. "Here you are."

She walked into the small, charming room that usually offered a view of orange-roofed villas and the blue sea. But right now there was nothing but darkness and the heavy beating of rain outside the deep-set window.

Automatically, she pointed to a small door in the plastered stone wall. "There's a bathroom through there. If you need anything, don't hesitate to ask."

She knew she sounded like a robot. It was bizarre, this feeling of standing outside herself and watching herself go through the motions of civility. "Just make your way back to the living room when you're done and we'll have a bite to eat. No need to rush."

As she went to walk out, Nikki put a hand on her arm to stop her. "Claire..."

She paused and half turned to look dispassionately at the other woman, as if she was looking at her from miles away.

Nikki continued quietly. "As far as I'm concerned, Luke's life was too high a price to pay for a scumbag like Espinoza. Luke was a decent man, one of the nicest I ever had the pleasure to work with. And...I think...he really cared about you."

She nodded numbly. Nikki was only trying to be kind. The worst of it was, she didn't even have the right to mourn him. They were just two strangers who'd shared a fleeting interlude. The brutal truth mocked the terrible emptiness inside her.

"If you'd like to know anything about him I'd be glad to answer any questions."

She could see the pain and compassion in Nikki's green eyes and felt grateful that the other woman seemed to not only understand her feelings but her needs.

"Thanks," she said quietly. "I'd appreciate that. Maybe a little later though." Right now she just had to be alone.

INSTEAD OF THE SOLITUDE she craved, Claire spent the rest of the day with her father and Nikki as the storm raged outside. Being alone left her prey to her memories, crowding in on her thick and fast and excruciatingly painful.

After lunch, James took their guest around the plushly restored medieval château and showed her his collections of silver and treasured antiques.

No one spoke about what had happened and the underlying strain made conversation brittle. But right now, Claire couldn't bear to know how it had happened and Nikki obviously didn't want to talk about it.

Why couldn't this be a dream, something she could wake from? But Claire knew, with devastating certainty that tomorrow would dawn and Luke would still be gone. This world would continue without him. Forever.

They said life went on, and it did, but right now she didn't care if it went on with or without her. If she'd ever doubted that what she felt was really love, that doubt had been irrevocably and brutally put to rest.

She knew now, now when it was too late, that she loved him, really loved him. Why hadn't she told him she'd loved him when she'd had the chance?

Finally it was time for bed. She dreaded it. There'd be no sleep for her tonight. As the dark closed in she lay beneath the covers, her body sagging into the mattress like a deadweight as the smothering blanket seemed to press her down onto the bed.

The rain had stopped, but through the window she could hear the drip, drip, drip of the water from the eaves. Her throat tightened and she closed her eyes. They burned, but the tears refused to come. Inside she felt dead. Would it be like this forever? Forever... How was she going to face forever when she couldn't even stand one more second of this paralyzing horror?

She opened her eyes and sat up, then let out a gasp. Faintly visible was the outline of a man standing at the foot of her bed. *Oh, God.* Was this some cruel, taunting hallucination?

"Luke." The anguished whisper tore out of her, knowing that this was the point where the vision would evaporate.

"Yes, it's me, Claire, love." His soft voice reached out to her through the darkness.

She stared up at the dim, familiar shape in the dark. A cool, tingling feeling suddenly rushed to her head and everything faded into utter blackness.

HER EYES FLUTTERED open to the soft light from her bedside lamp and Nikki's face loomed above her. She could feel her patting her left hand and turned to see her father on her right, holding her other hand.

"I had the strangest dream..." she began, looking from one set of anxious eyes to the other. "I dreamt that Luke was here. Standing right there at the bottom of my bed."

She saw James and Nikki exchange strange glances, then her father said gently, "That was no dream."

She followed his gaze and turned to look up and behind her, into the dim corner at the head of her bed.

He moved slowly into the nimbus of light from the lamp as she scrambled to her knees on the bed.

"Luke?" Her voice emerged a broken whisper.

"I'm sorry I frightened you like that." He paused in front of her, uncertainty in his eyes, as if holding himself back.

Joy went bubbling through her. "You fool, as if I care. It's you!" Half laughing, half crying, she launched herself at him and threw her arms tightly around his neck.

After a moment his arms came around her and squeezed her close. She felt him chuckling before she heard the deep, low rumble of his laughter. "Yes, it's me."

LESS THAN HALF an hour later they were all ensconced in deep wingback chairs in front of the library fireplace, each holding a snifter of brandy. The flames crackled around the sweet-smelling applewood logs, sending out a welcome glow of heat as the rain picked up again and beat against the window.

No sound had ever been so sweet to her before. He was alive! Her body sang with a joy more intense than she could ever have believed herself capable.

In the orange light Nikki's face shone with pleasure and tired relief. While more self-contained, James's quiet smile betrayed his delighted satisfaction.

Claire cradled her brandy, cuddling into the soft down-filled cushions and infused with a warmth so different from the deathly cold that had numbed her before. She couldn't take her eyes off Luke, lovingly tracing his features bronzed by the firelight. Her heart contracted to see a livid bruise spread along one cheekbone and the small cut above his left eye.

While the fire crackled and the rain beat steadily outside, Luke began to tell his story in a quiet, straightforward way.

"I was able to take Voorhees's place and arrived at Espinoza's island by launch. But before the team got there Espinoza had been warned of the raid. He took a Jeep and headed for the other side of the island.

"I took another Jeep and followed. I managed to cut him off on a mountain road and sent him into a ravine, but he escaped. I caught up with him and we had a bit of a tussle."

Claire bit her lip, he was downplaying any suggestion of heroics, but she could read between the lines all too clearly.

"Espinoza was getting the better of me," he said wryly. "And we weren't in the best of spots—it was a high bluff above a river. I was bound and determined that if I ended up in the river he was coming with me, and that's what happened. I landed in the water and got knocked unconscious. When I woke up I found myself wedged among some boulders in midstream, almost completely submerged. I suppose I was lucky I didn't drown."

Anxiety made her heart palpitate as she realized how close he'd come to dying. She felt the overwhelming desire to put her arms around him and never let him go, to guard him from pain and danger for the rest of her life. But she just sat, cradling her glass, her muscles tense as she listened to him talk.

"I got to shore, but there was no sign of Espinoza. When I got back to the compound I found it burned to the ground and absolutely deserted. That's when I realized that I'd probably been presumed dead.

"I found a launch and headed for the nearest island but I ran out of gas. Eventually I was picked up by a couple of young chaps who were kind enough to take me to Grenada.

"The first thing I did was call you." He held her gaze, his eyes glowing with the firelight. "I didn't know your number at home, so I called the auction house. Your boss sounded like quite a character." His mouth curved in a smile. "But anyway, I found out you'd extended your leave to visit your father at home."

Claire blushed, but fortunately he didn't ask her why.

"Next I tried here, but the lines were down. The flight back to Paris was the most frustrating time I've ever had. I called headquarters, and found out that Nikki had come up here to give James the coronet, but hadn't checked in since then.

"In Paris I had to charter a small plane to bring me on to Cannes. I couldn't wait for the regularly scheduled flight. Then I rented a car and drove up as far as I could before the road was washed out. I walked the rest of the way, only to find the damn gates locked. Why do they lock the gates around here?"

"Tradition, my boy." James sat back in his chair, swirling the brandy in his glass. "Tradition."

Luke smiled. "Anyway, I climbed the gates and broke into the château. End of story. By the way, I'm sorry about the lock on the terrace door."

"Did you pick it, or break it?" James asked idly.

"Let's just say, I *persuaded* it."

James gave a long-suffering sigh. "Albert will have to take care of it in the morning."

"And that brings me to the reason why I came." Turning his gaze back to her, she met his eyes, now dark and serious.

She swallowed, suddenly filled with breathless anxiety. "Well, I'm sure those reasons can wait until after you've had a good night's sleep. You must be exhausted."

"Oh, no, you don't." He pinned her with his relentless gaze. "I have literally been through hell and high water to see you, to talk to you, and you're not going to pack me off to bed before I've done that."

"That's not necessary. We don't have to talk about anything. I understand everything perfectly well."

"And what exactly do you understand so well?" he said quietly.

She looked down at the Aubusson carpet, unable to meet his eyes a second longer. "Well . . . we had a wonderful time together. It was a fantasy come true. I think we both enjoyed ourselves. I don't regret anything, but it's over."

The sudden complete silence was broken only by the hiss of logs in the grate. Claire looked up to find something in Luke's expression that made the blood begin to pound in her veins.

"And that's all? All there is for you?" The flames danced and flickered, reflected in his pale wolf eyes.

"Of course."

"Are you sure? Because there's a heck of a lot more to it for me."

Her mouth went dry, but this time she knew better than to let her feelings sweep her away. Luke was probably still carrying a sense of guilt, a sense of responsibility that she'd felt used. That was all. And she shouldn't read anything into it.

Most of all, though, the man had just faced death. Was it any wonder he'd cling misguidedly to the heightened emotions that had taken both of them by storm? But they'd been an illusion, and he was mistaking them for something deeper.

"How can there be?" she said gently. "We're strangers to each other. Those three days we shared had nothing to do with real life, we were both acting a part."

"Were you acting a part all the time, even when we were making love?" His face tightened with intensity. "Was that someone else?"

"No...yes..." Her fingers tightened around the stem of the glass in confusion. "How do I know? I've never felt that way before, I've never acted that way before. I don't know who that person was."

"Well, I know how I felt, and what I felt was real." The firelight bronzed the taut lines of his face, his voice hard and intense. "And no, I'd never felt that way before, or acted that way before, either. It was no act."

All at once she became aware of James and Nikki watching them. She'd been so caught up she'd forgotten they were even there. Nikki's mouth hung open in fascination, as if she were watching a movie, and James had a gleam in his eye, as if he was amused to see his daughter in this position.

Her cheeks flushed with more than the heat from the fire and she said quietly, "Maybe we should talk in the morning."

"No," Luke said forcefully. "We're going to settle it right now. I love you, Claire, marry me."

With a gasp, she put the brandy glass down on the small table next to her chair, her hands shaking badly, and turned to face him. "You're crazy! We've only known each other for three days. We're complete strangers."

"Some people can be strangers to each other after forty years." He leaned a little toward her, his pale eyes boring into her. "Do you love me?"

"No," she snapped.

James coughed. "Well, that's a lie," her father said laconically, and she darted him a furious glance. "You told me you loved him."

"She told you she loved me?" Luke turned avidly to James. "When?"

"Before we left Bateaux." Her father stroked his neat beard and gave her a piercing look.

"I was distraught and confused..." she began, then her voice hardened. "And you told me I was a fool for falling in love with a virtual stranger! So you keep out of this. Whose side are you on, anyway? Do you actually want me to marry a man I don't know?"

James's dark brows rose eloquently. "Didn't stop you from sleeping with him."

Another rush of heat flooded her cheeks. "That was different."

"Oh, yes, that goes without saying." On that dry, sarcastic murmur James took another sip of his brandy.

"Claire..." Luke's voice wrapped around her heart, soft, deep and coaxing, as warm and rich as chocolate brown velvet. She turned her gaze to him and found his eyes sparkling with an intense fire of sincerity that had nothing to do with the reflected flames. "You *do* love me, I know you do. Do you think I can't feel it?"

"But... but we've only known each other for three days. How can we trust feelings that bloomed in such an unreal situation? I don't even know anything about you." Why couldn't he see this was crazy? "I can understand now why you could say so little about yourself, of course. And I also understand your fascination with my background," she added dryly.

"That only accounted for half of my fascination. The other half was wanting to know more about the woman who had stolen my heart. You walked into my life and that was it."

"But..."

"Do you think it was easy falling in love with you while believing you to be a thief? Trying to figure out how I could have you and reconcile that with my ethics?" His voice took on a hard edge of self-condemnation. "For God's sake, I even found myself thinking of ways to shield you from the law. Does that sound like I wasn't serious in the way I felt?"

With every atom of her being she longed to believe, but... "What about the fact we live an ocean apart? And... and your job. I don't know how I would feel about you facing that kind of danger all the time."

"So is that the real reason? You won't have me because of the job I do?" Quiet and intense, he waited for her answer, his eyes dark and serious.

"No," she confessed. "That's not the reason. I wouldn't let your job stand in the way. If I married you, I'd accept you the way you are—job and all."

His face cleared. "I'm glad to hear it." He eased back in the chair a little. "Nevertheless, I'm giving up my job."

Her mouth fell open in horror. "I couldn't let you do that! Guaranteed, after a while you'd start resenting me."

"That's not true. Do you think if I had you, I'd want a job that would take me away from you all the time? Let alone risk my life. Besides, for a while now I've been feeling that it's time for me to make a change. I'm losing my edge..."

"No, you're not!" she protested. "From everything I've seen you still have what it takes."

He shook his head. "No, Claire, I'm getting too old for this job." He gave a wry smile. "But it wasn't till I met you and fell in love with you that I started to feel the need to have a life of my own. You don't know how happy my mother will be."

His expression became earnest. "I still believe in what I'm doing, and as long as there are people like Espinoza around there'll be a need for people to stop them. I can still do that, but in a less active way."

"But—"

He cut her off. "And don't imagine that I would be sacrificing a good job, either. I think I could land something even better, with all my seniority in the agency. Now here's where the compromise comes in, Claire—you'd have to move to London. But I think with your expertise you wouldn't have much trouble finding work."

Dazedly, she shook her head. He was going too fast, and making it sound so perfectly simple and reasonable but... "It still doesn't alter the fact that we've only known each other for three days," she protested, trying to be the voice of sanity, trying to prevent herself from being drawn back into the fantasy.

"So that's it, then? If that's the only drawback..." He crossed his arms and settled back into the chair, looking as if he were there for the winter. "Then I'm just going to stay right here and tell you every minute, boring detail of my life until you feel you know me well enough for you to marry me."

"Here!" James sat up in alarm. "Now just a minute..."

"You're crazy!" Claire gasped.

But part of her wanted to believe she could push away all the sensible objections and follow this mad scheme.

"Mmm-hmm..." Luke nodded his head. "Yes, I am. About you." The corners of his mouth curved in the hint of a smile. "Don't you see, we just did it backward, that's all. We fell in love first, and now we're going to spend the rest of our lives getting to know each other."

Claire looked at him helplessly for a moment, then glanced at the others. With a mixture of awe and amusement, Nikki gave her an encouraging nod.

James still had that look of disgust at the notion of Luke moving in, but at the same time she could see he respected and approved of the man.

Her gaze turned to Luke, who just sat watching her, and she knew there'd be no more coaxing, no more pressure.

She took a big, shuddering breath. "I hope we're not making a big mistake." Her voice faltered as Luke's eyes took on a gleam of triumph. "I'm not sure I'm equipped to deal with the problems that could arise."

"No worry about that." His eyes glowed and she could hear the vibrant hum of suppressed laughter in his voice. "After all, that's my specialty. I guess you could say I'm a sort of a problem solver."

"Yes, like you solved the problem of Enrico Espinoza." She gave him a wry smile, but inside she was trembling.

He rose to his feet with that swift economic grace she loved and came over to her. Slowly he pulled her up and wrapped his arms around her waist.

"Quit stalling," he murmured. "Just tell me that you love me and you'll marry me, because I'm very tired and I want to go to bed." He smiled with the teasing words, but when she looked into his eyes all she saw there was love and need and desire. And a promise that took her breath away.

"I love you, and I'll marry you," she said simply, and wondered if it were possible to die from happiness.

For a moment he just looked at her, then his shoulders sagged as he let out a sigh. "Thank God for that." He pulled her close and held her tightly against him.

"Amen!" James put his snifter down with a definite clink. "Now, can we all go to bed?"

Luke murmured against her hair. "That's the best offer I've had all night." He raised his head and turned to James. "I hope you don't expect us to inhabit separate bedrooms until the wedding."

Claire turned in time to catch her father's dry look. "Would it matter if I did?"

"Not one bit," Luke said firmly.

"That's what I thought." James heaved a long-suffering sigh.

"I suppose I should call you Dad now," Luke said with a straight face.

James shuddered. "Good Lord, surely there's no need."

Luke chuckled, a deep rumble that vibrated through her body as he held her tight against him. He let her go, took her by the hand and headed for the door.

Bemused, she looked back to see Nikki, grinning from ear to ear. And James, with a warm twinkle of approbation in his eye that told her he heartily approved.

"Good night," she flung over her shoulder as Luke pulled her impatiently out of the room.

As they headed out into the hall she heard Nikki breathe, "God, that was romantic." Then her voice softened and took on a provocative note. "So, James...how do you feel about taking up where we had to so rudely leave off the other night?"

"Young lady, don't you think I'm too old for you?"

Claire smiled. The vain, old peacock, brazenly fishing.

"I like my men with experience," Nikki said seductively.

"Hmm..."

She knew that dubious response all too well. He hadn't got the reply he'd been angling for.

But then his humor swiftly reasserted itself as he gave a soft, wicked chuckle. "Well, I have plenty of that."

As Luke pulled her urgently up the stairs, Claire smiled to herself. The incorrigible old rogue. Albert would have a field day with this one.

LUKE PULLED HER into her room. The small lamp was still burning by the bed, leaving the corners and the beamed ceiling swathed in shadows. He closed the door behind them with a soft click. She turned to face him, suddenly shy, and looked down at their clasped hands.

This wasn't a dazzling fantasy played out in an anonymous hotel. Now this was her real life, her room, breathtakingly quiet except for the irregular liquid splash of rain on the windowsill. And now there was no one else's presence to dilute the wildfire of need and emotion burning between them.

Everything that required saying had been said. Everything else could wait for tomorrow. Right now she just needed to be with him, this man she'd fallen in love with in the most unbelievable, inexplicable way.

But she could see the shadow of uncertainty in his eyes. He was waiting for her to make the first move. "Have I... bullied you into this?" he asked slowly. "I want you to come to me of your own free will, because you love me and have no reservations. Not just because I pressured you."

In the hard, uncompromising lines of his face she saw everything about him. The way he approached life head-on. The high standards he lived by, and his honesty. Most of all, she could see his love for her.

"Three days isn't a lot of time in which to fall in love." Her voice was a whisper in the quiet room. "But I know I've never felt this way before. So how do I know it's love? I don't. But I do know that when I'm with you I feel whole. When I thought you were dead..." A shudder tore through her and his hands tightened on hers. "Something in me died, too."

"I'm not dead," he said softly. "I'm very much alive, and I love you very much."

"Then what more could I ask for?"

In an instant she had closed the gap between them and reached up for his mouth. The moment his lips touched hers she gasped at the rush of desire blazing through her. She wrapped her arms around him, but he winced and groaned.

She moved away a fraction and looked up at him in alarm. "What's the matter?"

"Just a few scrapes and bruises here and there." He bent his head to kiss her again, but she pulled back.

"Scrapes and bruises, what from?"

He chuckled. "Claire, the man wasn't exactly teaching me how to tango, he was beating the hell out of me. And I was doing my best to stop him."

The rueful amusement in his face didn't dispel her sudden horror as the meaning sank in. "Oh, my God! Oh, my God, Luke."

She'd listened to him recite that catalog of trials he'd endured and he'd made it sound so prosaic that she'd never stopped to think how badly he'd been hurt.

Slowly, stiffly, he began to take off his jacket and she grabbed onto the lapels. "Here, let me help you."

She saw him wince as his shoulder muscles flexed. Tugging his black turtleneck free of the jeans, she pulled it up and gasped in horror to see a gauze dressing barely covering a massive gash down his side. Gently pulling the turtleneck off over his head, she saw an ugly bruise discoloring his left shoulder.

Her face must have betrayed the sick pain she felt. Luke said casually, "It looks a lot worse than it really is."

She gave him a fierce look. "Don't lie to me."

"You're right." He let out a plaintive sigh. "I'm definitely in need of a lot of tender loving care."

"And don't be funny at a time like this." She reached out and tentatively touched the dark purple bruise with her fingertips. "*This* isn't anything to joke about. How on earth did you make it back?"

"I thought of you," he said simply.

The depth and force of the love she saw in his face brought a sudden stinging rush of tears to her eyes.

"I promised you I'd come back," Luke said softly. "And I always keep my promises. And now I promise to love you till the day I die."

She blinked away the tears. "And I do love you." Lifting her face to his again, she whispered against his mouth the timeless words of Elizabeth Barrett Browning who had loved the way she loved Luke. "'I love thee with the breath/Smiles, tears, of all my life!—and if God choose/I shall but love thee better after death.'"

Taking his hand, she led him over to the bed, sat him down and gently pushed him back against the pillows. Then slowly, carefully, she removed the rest of his clothes while he watched her with lazy contentment. The satisfied repose of a man who had labored long and hard to earn his rest.

A wellspring of nurturing tenderness rushed through her. The knowledge that he was hers to love and care for, for the rest of her life. And she was his.

After undressing him, she got into bed beside him and snuggled up close, being careful not to hurt him. She turned into his arms and met his gently seeking mouth.

"Let's live happily ever after," she breathed against his lips and felt them curve into a smile, then heard the devilish humor in his seductive growl.

"Let's!"

MILLS & BOON

Weddings ❖ Glamour ❖ Family ❖ Heartbreak

Weddings By DeWilde

Since the turn of the century, the elegant and fashionable DeWilde stores have helped brides around the world realise the fantasy of their 'special day'.

Now the store and three generations of the DeWilde family are torn apart by the separation of Grace and Jeffrey DeWilde—and family members face new challenges and loves in this fast-paced, glamourous, internationally set series.

For weddings, romance and glamour, enter the world of

Weddings By DeWilde

—a fantastic line up of 12 new stories from popular **Mills & Boon authors**

NOVEMBER 1996

Bk. 3 DRESSED TO THRILL - Kate Hoffmann
Bk. 4 WILDE HEART - Daphne Clair

Available from WH Smith, John Menzies, Volume One, Forbuoys, Martins, Woolworths, Tesco, Asda, Safeway and other paperback stockists.

MILLS & BOON

Temptation

the wrong bed

The Wrong Bed!
The Wrong Man!
The Ultimate Disaster!

Dee Ann Karenbrock had hit rock bottom. Her fiancé had left her at the altar and then had the nerve to invite her to his wedding—to his ex-wife. Could it get any worse? But Dee Ann's nightmare had just begun. Because the next morning, she woke up adrift and naked with her worst enemy, Julian Wainright!

Don't miss this fabulous mini-series from Temptation—1 book a month for 5 months—starting with...

Bedded Bliss by Heather MacAllister in November '96

THE FAMILY WAY
Jayne Ann Krentz

Having a baby was supposed to be a joyous occasion, but Pru Kenyon wasn't smiling. True, her relationship with live-in lover Case McCord was both electrifying and deeply satisfying, but she didn't have the benefit of a ring on her finger...

Pru wasn't about to force Case's hand—she knew he'd propose out of a sense of duty, rather than love. And if she couldn't have his love, then she didn't want him...

"It's no wonder that the author's novels consistently hit bestseller lists."

Publisher's Weekly

MIRA®

This month's
irresistible novels from

Temptation

TO CATCH A THIEF by Debra Carroll

Vulnerable but determined Claire Sterling is searching for her father—not a handsome but dangerous lover. But when incredibly sexy Luke Dalton holds her in his arms, Claire discovers passion *and* mystery. Because like her, he too is hiding secrets—he's searching for her father for reasons of his own...

MICHAEL'S ANGEL by Lyn Ellis

Michael Weldon had the perfect life, complete with a sexy, loving wife, Terri and a terrific son, Josh. But then Josh died. And Michael walked out, leaving Terri to deal with her grief alone. But just when Michael thought it was all over, his guardian angel came to him, bringing a message of hope...

THE STORMCHASER by Rita Clay Estrada

Rebels & Rogues

Cane Mitchell's job, his whole life, was to go where the danger was. Fires, floods, tornadoes, tidal waves—he'd be there. But when he met gentle Bernadette Conrad, he wanted to run like mad!

IMPETUOUS by Lori Foster

On the outside, Carlie McDaniels was a shy no-nonsense schoolteacher. But on the inside, there was another Carlie—a sultry, sexy femme fatale—burning to get out. One night, she did. And lady-killer Tyler Ramsey didn't know what hit him!

Spoil yourself next month
with these four novels from

Temptation

THE MARRIAGE CURSE by Carolyn Andrews

Mattie Farrell wasn't going to be scared into leaving Barclayville—especially when the one doing the scaring was gorgeous Grant Whittaker. She was determined to make Barclay House into an inn—curse or no curse. But before long, Mattie began to question her plans—and her sizzling affair with Grant...

BEDDED BLISS by Heather MacAllister

The Wrong Bed

Dee Ann Karrenbrock had hit rock bottom. Her fiancé had left her at the altar and then had the nerve to invite her to his wedding—to his ex-wife. Dee Ann didn't think it could get any worse. But her nightmare had only just begun, because the next morning she woke up adrift, alone and naked with her worst enemy, Julian Wainright!

TOUCH THE HEAVENS by Eileen Nauman

Flying was her first passion...and then Chris Mallory met Major Dan McCord, her instructor in test-pilot school. In such a male-dominated field, Chris had enough to handle without beginning a love affair. But could she ignore the magical attraction between them?

THE COWBOY BY Kristine Rolofson

Rogues

Practical and organized Elizabeth Richards read all about outlaws like the Younger gang in an unusual old book. But when she woke up in bed with sexy Logan Younger—in 1886—she knew she was in big trouble!

MILLS & BOON

Celebrate the magic of Christmas!

With the Mills & Boon Christmas Gift Pack...

Mistletoe Magic

We've brought together four delightful romances from our bestselling authors especially for you this Christmas!

Her Christmas Fantasy
by **Penny Jordan**

Christmas Nights
by **Sally Wentworth**

A Mistletoe Marriage
by **Jeanne Allan**

Kissing Santa
by **Jessica Hart**

Special Christmas Price £6.30

GET 4 BOOKS AND A MYSTERY GIFT

FREE

Return this coupon and we'll send you 4 Mills & Boon Temptation® novels and a mystery gift absolutely FREE! We'll even pay the postage and packing for you.

We're making you this offer to introduce you to the benefits of Reader Service: FREE home delivery of brand-new Mills & Boon Temptation novels, at least a month before they are available in the shops, FREE gifts and a monthly Newsletter packed with information.

Accepting these FREE books and gift places you under no obligation to buy, you may cancel at any time, even after receiving just your free shipment. Simply complete the coupon below and send it to:

MILLS & BOON® READER SERVICE, FREEPOST, CROYDON, SURREY, CR9 3WZ.

No stamp needed

Yes, please send me 4 free Mills & Boon Temptation novels and a mystery gift. I understand that unless you hear from me, I will receive 4 superb new titles every month for just £2.10* each postage and packing free. I am under no obligation to purchase any books and I may cancel or suspend my subscription at any time, but the free books and gifts will be mine to keep in any case. (I am over 18 years of age)

T6JE

Ms/Mrs/Miss/Mr _____

Address _____

_____

_____ Postcode_____

Offer closes 30th April 1997. We reserve the right to refuse an application. *Prices and terms subject to change without notice. Offer only valid in UK and Ireland and is not available to current subscribers to this series. **Readers in Ireland please write to:** P.O. Box 4546, Dublin 24. Overseas readers please write for details.

You may be mailed with offers from other reputable companies as a result of this application. Please tick box if you would prefer not to receive such offers.

MILLS & BOON

Christmas Miracles

Christmas Miracles really can happen, as you'll find out in our festive collection of three heart-warming romantic stories from three of our most popular authors:

A Christmas Proposal ★ by **Betty Neels**

Heavenly Angels ★ by **Carole Mortimer**

A Daddy for Christmas ★ by **Rebecca Winters**

Available: November '96   Price: £4.99

Available from WH Smith, John Menzies, Volume One, Forbuoys, Martins, Woolworths, Tesco, Asda, Safeway and other paperback stockists.